CAPPUCCINOS AND CORPSES

CUP OF JO BOOK 2

KELLY HASHWAY

To Ayla with love

CHAPTER ONE

Not everyone gets a chance to start over in the place where they grew up, but I definitely have. And while it's a little weird being back in Bennett Falls and dealing with my ex, Detective Quentin Perry, and his fiancée, Samantha Shaw, whom I used to call my best friend, I can't complain too much. My coffee shop, Cup of Jo, has been up and running for one month, and it's been going surprisingly well—even after I stopped carrying baked goods made by my boyfriend, Camden Turner. Cam opened up his own bakery right next door to Cup of Jo and named it Cam's Kitchen. I helped him decorate and get the place ready, and now it's his turn to have a grand opening.

Since I'm not selling Cam's baked goods anymore, I'm selling chocolates. Coffee and chocolates—seriously, does it get any better than that? I bought an insane amount of chocolate molds, and I melt and remold the chocolates myself. It couldn't be easier, and they're a huge hit.

So, I have no complaints when I walk into work Monday morning to start another week.

My younger sister, Maura, or Mo as everyone calls her, comes walking into Cup of Jo the second I unlock the doors.

"Coffee. Now. Didn't sleep. Just inject it straight into my veins, please." She pulls up the sleeve of her sweater to expose her arm.

"Stop it. You hate needles. Why would you even suggest such a thing?"

"No sleep." She slumps into a chair at one of the tables, places her arms out as a pillow, and lowers her head onto them.

"Why didn't you sleep?" I ask, setting up my coffee machines for the day.

"Lance."

Despite having grown up with nothing after his father left him and his mother penniless, Lance Tunney is opening up an upscale restaurant this Friday. He happens to be a good friend of my neighbor Jamar, and I also gave Lance an inheritance check I recently received. The guy's had a rough life, and now that his mother is in prison, he needs all the friends he can get.

"Is everything okay?" I ask.

She raises her head slightly. "Yes, he's just freaking out about the grand opening. Wait until you see him.

Total makeover, thanks to me. New haircut, new clothes, new everything." She waves a hand in the direction of the coffeemakers. "Chop, chop. I'm dying over here."

"Do you want a cappuccino? It's today's special, or it will be once I write out the specials board." I have one of those cute blackboard specials menus, and I draw a picture of the featured coffee of the day on it. My entire shop is black and white to complement my blackboard menu theme. The one on the long back wall displays every type and flavor of coffee on offer. But I bring plenty of pops of color with the neon chalk I use.

"Don't care. Just need caffeine," Mo whines.

I roll my eyes and start making her cappuccino. "You definitely weren't giving him a makeover last night, so what were you doing that kept you from sleeping?"

"Designing ads for him."

"Are you still working pro bono?" I ask as I finish steaming the milk.

"No, he's paying me now that he has the money to do so, but I'm not charging him anywhere near my usual rate."

"Good for you, Mo."

"Yeah, I'm an angel. That's what he keeps telling me, anyway. How's my coffee coming along?"

"The perfect cappuccino can't be rushed. I'm making the espresso now."

"Ugh." She lets out a moan and lowers her head to the table.

About a minute later, the door of the shop opens, and I turn to see Cam walking in.

"What's going on in here? It sounded like someone was dying." His gaze goes to Mo.

"I am," she whines.

I smile at Cam. We've known each other all our lives, but it wasn't until about four weeks ago that we finally admitted we were more than best friends. "Hey, you. Are you ready for your big opening?" I top off Mo's cappuccino with perfectly balanced layers of steamed milk and foam before handing it to her.

She grabs it, doesn't say thank you, and immediately takes a sip, pulling away with a foam mustache. I don't bother telling her. "I have to go to work. See you in about an hour when I need another fix." She stands up and raises the to-go cup to me.

Cam wags a finger at Mo. "Um, you—"

I shake my head at Cam.

"Yes?" she asks him.

"You have a good day," he says with a smile.

She grunts in response and walks out.

Cam laughs and walks to the counter to greet me with a proper kiss hello. "What did she do to make you think she should be embarrassed at work with a milk moustache?"

"Forgot to thank me for the cappuccino. You want one?"

"Yes but no. I just wanted to say good morning before I open the doors to start the day."

"If I get a moment, I'll bring a cappuccino to you, but since I plan to send all my customers to Cam's Kitchen from here, you might not get a second to drink it."

He rests his hands on my hips and gives me a gentle squeeze. "I hope I'm that busy, but I'm not going to hold my breath. A few business owners aren't exactly happy with me now that I'm not baking for them anymore."

"Hey, I found a way to get by without your baked goods. They will, too," I say.

His eyes go to the dark chocolate sticks I have individually wrapped on the counter next to the black and white mug for tips that Cam gave me as a present at my own grand opening. "You put out the chocolate sticks."

"Yeah, I'm trying them out for the first time today." The point is to put them directly in your coffee cup and let them melt. "I'm hoping they'll be a big hit like the other chocolates I make."

"Okay, I'm definitely coming in at some point to get one of those."

I rub his arms. "Don't be nervous. Today is going to be great. You'll see. And to get ready…" I hold up one finger and disappear behind the counter. I return with a cookie jar that says "Tips" on it. "I thought it was only fitting to get you a tip jar since you bought one for me."

He takes the tip jar and kisses me. "Thank you. I love it. I'll put it on the counter by my register." He looks behind him at the coffee cup clock on the wall. "I should go. Wish me luck."

"You're not going to need it, but good luck." I watch him walk outside, and then I turn my own closed sign around to let everyone know I'm open for the day.

Cynthia Townsend, a local music teacher at the high school, is my first customer. She looks like she's in a big hurry, and I can't help wondering why she's rushing so much when the high school is only two miles away. She has plenty of time to make it before her first class begins.

"Good morning, Cynthia," I say. "Can I interest you in a cappuccino?" I realize I still haven't written out the specials board since I had visitors this morning.

"Two please." She looks back over her right shoulder.

"Are you okay?" I ask her.

"Yeah, just in a hurry. Will is waiting outside."

I get started on the cappuccinos. "Early meeting before classes?" I ask.

"Yeah, and we've been having trouble with the car. Something with the brakes. Will brought it in to have the brakes changed over the weekend. We're picking it up from the mechanic on Second Street. It's rotten luck since my car is completely dead."

"Oh, I'm sorry to hear that. Did you walk this morning then?" I ask, knowing they live in a tiny two-bedroom cottage on the other side of the park.

"A friend dropped us off."

I finish fixing both drinks and place the to-go cups on

the counter. "You and Will should check out Cam's Kitchen. He just opened today."

"Maybe another day." Cynthia hands me a twenty-dollar bill, and as I start to ring her up, she backs up, saying, "Keep the change. I've got to go."

"But…" She's already gone before I can protest. Why would someone who needs a new car leave me a tip that's larger than her bill? I put the money aside, resigned to giving it to her later when she's not in such a hurry. Then I get to work on the specials board.

I'm just finishing up when the sound of sirens fills the air. I look up to see an ambulance speed down Main Street. I put the board down next to the counter and step outside. Cam is at his door to my right, and he steps outside when he sees me.

"It turned onto Second Street," he says.

My ex best friend, Samantha, comes rushing across the street. She hurries over to us since her flower shop, Bouquets of Love, is on the other side of Cup of Jo.

"What's going on over there?" I ask Samantha.

"There was a car accident on Second Street. Officer Stiles blocked off the road. He said two people were killed."

"Do you know who it is?" Being that her fiancé is a police detective, Samantha has a way of finding out more than she should in situations like this.

"Cynthia and William Townsend."

My jaw drops. "Cynthia was just here," I say.

"I know. I saw her and Will leave. That's the second time in under a month that someone died after leaving your coffee shop, Jo. It's like you're cursed or something."

She might be right. I seem to be doomed to be interrogated by my ex in connection to people's deaths.

CHAPTER TWO

With all the commotion on the street, a crowd begins to form. Several people decide to come inside Cup of Jo since my shop has a good view and they can get their caffeine fixes.

Cam nods. "Go on. You have customers."

I feel bad that no one seems to be going inside his bakery. I give his hand a squeeze before entering my shop. I managed to fit two more tables in here since opening, and now all six tables are fully occupied.

I move behind the counter and take the first order before calling out, "If anyone is hungry, Cam's Kitchen is open next door. Feel free to go buy some baked goods while I make your coffees." A few people take me up on that, and I breathe a sigh of relief. I don't want Cam's opening day to be a flop, especially when I was the one who kept telling him to take the plunge and open his own bakery.

I'm amazed by the amount of buzz concerning the accident since it doesn't seem like anyone here actually witnessed it. But considering Cup of Jo became the place to be after I was involved in a murder investigation about four weeks ago, I'm not all that surprised. This town loves to gossip.

"I heard the car went right into that empty space Cam Turner used to lease for his kitchen," Mickey Baldwin says. He might be more of a gossip than the little old ladies who spend their days with their noses pressed to store windows to try to see what everyone is up to.

"Who did you hear that from?" I ask, handing him his cappuccino.

"I heard the police mention it on my way here. I was just at Cam's Kitchen telling him about it. Good thing he opened his own place, or there might be another dead body to bury."

At this point, everyone in town knows about Cam and me, so I can't believe Mickey is being so nonchalant talking about Cam dying.

Sheila Marks smacks his arm. "Mickey, Cam is Jo's boyfriend. Don't say things like that to her."

"What? I said I'm glad Cam wasn't hurt."

"It's okay," I say. "I know you meant well."

Sheila offers me a sympathetic smile. "Think Cam will be upset? I mean he operated out of that space for about five years. It must hold a lot of memories for him."

"I think he'll be okay. Like Mickey said, at least he's

here on Main Street now and wasn't in the path of that car."

"Do they have any idea what caused the accident?" Sheila asks, but Mickey just shrugs.

"I know," Samantha says from behind me, making me jump. "You're jumpy, Jo," she says.

"When did you come in? Who's watching your flower shop?" I ask.

She waves a hand in the air. "It's fine. I put a sign on my door that I was over here. If anyone needs me, they can just come here."

Great. When I leased the space next to her shop, I had no idea she'd want to spend so much time here, but she hasn't exactly figured out that we're no longer friends after she betrayed me. I've come to terms with her and Quentin, and part of me is glad I saw what kind of person Quentin is before I wound up engaged to him, but I don't exactly want to socialize with either of them.

Now, if only someone would tell them that.

As if he senses I'm thinking about him, Quentin walks into the coffee shop. He makes a beeline for Samantha and me, wrapping an arm around Sam.

Everyone stops talking, waiting for Quentin to fill them in.

"I figured this is where I'd find a large group of people," he begins. "Let me start by saying you're all aware of the amount of rain we had last night. Second Street is having a drainage issue, and it caused part of the road to flood. We're certain Mr. Townsend simply hydroplaned, causing him to lose control of the vehicle and crash into the storefront. No one else was injured since the space is currently sitting empty. It was an unfortunate accident, but an accident nonetheless."

A few people start asking questions, but Quentin holds up a hand and says, "That's all I can say about the matter at this time. Sorry, folks." He walks up to the counter, which forces me to follow.

"What can I get for you, Detective?"

He looks down at the specials board. "I'll take a cappuccino to go."

"Heading back to the station?" I ask as I get started on his drink.

"Yeah. It should be a simple open-and-closed case, though." He laughs, which makes me turn my head to look at him because I can't see what's amusing about two people dying. "Sorry, I don't mean to be insensitive. It's just that we found two to-go cups in the vehicle. From Cup of Jo, which I'm sure you already know about."

"I do. Cynthia was in here this morning." I finish making the drink, debating if I should tell Quentin about Cynthia's strange behavior. He's probably right. It was probably an accident caused by the flooded road, but something about the way Cynthia seemed in a rush and almost like someone was watching her or following her makes me give in and talk. "Quentin, Cynthia was acting odd when she was here."

"Odd how?"

"Well, she kept looking over her shoulder."

"Probably because Will was waiting for her outside," Samantha says, still at Quentin's side, her arm looped through his. "I saw him."

"Well, there you go," Quentin says, easily dismissing my concern because the love of his life said as much.

"Right but she was in a hurry. I mean, she said she had a meeting before her first class, but she paid with a twenty and told me to keep the change." I cap his drink and put it on the counter before reaching into the register to pull out the twenty-dollar bill I put under the drawer for safe keeping. "I was planning to give her the change later because she said her car died and Will's was having trouble with the brakes. They were on their way to pick it up from the mechanic on Second Street."

"They still had to pick up their car before heading to their meeting. They were in a hurry, so they probably didn't notice the standing water before it was too late," Quentin says before sipping his cappuccino. "This is really good." He hands me a ten-dollar bill, and I give him his change.

"I know that, but I can't help feeling like something was wrong."

Quentin puts his change in his wallet. "Look, Jo, you did a great job helping me on that last case, but it's time to put away your *invisible badge*—I believe you called it."

"But what if there's more to this?"

"Then that's for the police to figure out." He gives me a nod, and he and Samantha walk out, still arm in arm.

13

I'd feel a lot better if I thought he was actually going to look into the accident, but I know he won't.

At lunchtime, Mo comes in to the shop with her hand outstretched. She doesn't look any more awake than she did first thing this morning. I make her a double espresso, which she downs as quickly as possible without totally scorching her mouth.

"Go next door, and buy something from Cam," I tell her after handing her a refill.

"I don't have any money on me," she says. "I left my wallet at home."

I reach into the register and pull out a twenty-dollar bill. "Don't come back with change, and do not tell him I gave that to you."

"Yes, Mom," she says. "But I'm finishing this first." She takes another sip of the double espresso. "I'm assuming you heard about the accident."

"Yeah, except I'm not convinced it was an accident."

"Why not?" she asks, taking another sip.

"I don't know. It's just a feeling I have. Want to come over for dinner and help me figure out what's bothering me about it?"

"Depends. What will you be feeding me?"

"I'm making calzone. The dough is currently rising on my counter as we speak."

She rubs her stomach. "Yum. I love your calzone. Pepperoni and broccoli?" she asks.

I nod.

"I'm so there. But promise you and Cam won't be all

disgustingly coupley. It's been a while since I've been on a date, and I'm in that *I hate all couples* stage right now."

"Need I remind you that you pushed for Cam and me to get together in the first place?" I lean my elbows on the countertop.

"No, and I'm totally happy for you guys. I just don't want to see all the gag-worthy sweetness. I have to watch Quentin and Sam every morning from my office window. It's—" She cuts herself off. "Oh, Jo, I'm sorry. That was really insensitive of me."

"No, it's fine. I'm over that. Really. Quentin has nothing on Cam, and I agree that Quentin and Samantha can be truly vomit-inducing sometimes."

She pats my hand, finishes the double espresso, and pushes the empty cup toward me. "I'll take a cappuccino with one of those chocolate sticks in it when I get back from Cam's. Do you want anything?" She holds up the twenty-dollar bill. "It's your money after all."

"I'll take a piece of crumb cake."

"You got it." She turns to leave, and I get to work on the cappuccino.

"Hey, Jo," Samantha says, marching right up to the counter. Does she ever work? I feel like she's always here.

"What can I get for you, Samantha?" I ask, trying not to sound as annoyed as I feel, which is pretty much the usual when I'm around her.

"Oh, nothing, actually. I'm supposed to give you a message."

"From?" I finish steaming the milk for Mo's drink.

"Quentin. He said to tell you to 'stay out of this.'" She says the last part in a lower register. "He said that in his sexy, deep cop voice. You know the one. Oh, and he said figuring out one case doesn't make you a cop."

Quentin has no idea I helped solve a murder back in California before I returned to Bennett Falls. Not that I think it would make much difference in his mind. "Great. Thanks, Samantha. Anything else? I have customers waiting."

"Not right now. I'll be back later for my mid-afternoon coffee, though." She gives me a wave and leaves.

Oh joy. I'll get to see her again before my workday is over. Just what I want to hear.

Cam and I are both locking our doors at six o'clock. Since most of the town is going home for dinner, we don't bother staying open past six. Both of our businesses cater to the work crowd that ends their day at five.

"How was it?" I ask Cam. "Your coffee cake was delicious. I had Mo grab some for me when she said she was stopping in for lunch."

He wraps an arm around my waist as we walk toward my car. "Uh-huh. That was after you gave her money and told her to go to C.K.'s, right?"

Busted. Though knowing Mo, she caved and told him the truth the moment he got suspicious. "C.K.'s, I like that," I say, trying to steer the conversation in a different direction.

"Thanks, but you should know I didn't take your money."

I stop walking and face him. "What? Why not?"

"I'm not charging my girlfriend or her sister for food. You never charge me for coffee." I start to protest, but he holds up a finger. "It works both ways."

"Fine," I say, opening the door to my car. "So, Mo still has my twenty?"

He nods.

Of course, she tried to keep it. "I'll get it back at dinner. You want to come over? I'm making calzone."

"Sounds great. Give me a half hour."

"That works because I'll need at least forty-five minutes to prepare and cook the calzone once I'm home."

He gives me a kiss, but his face falls.

"What's wrong?" Was opening day that bad?

"I don't know why, but I hate that the space I used to rent now has a giant hole in the side of it. I spent five years there."

I place my hand on top of his on the car door. "I know."

"It's stupid because two people lost their lives, which is so much more important than losing a space where I used to bake."

"It's not stupid. It was important to you."

He lets go of the door. "Go on home. I'll see you in a bit."

I nod and watch him walk toward his car parked a little farther down the road. What are the odds that Cam's old kitchen would get destroyed less than a month after he left it? He might be right about it being small in comparison to the Townsends losing their lives, but I get an overwhelming urge to see the crime scene. I wait until Cam's car pulls out of the parking spot and onto the road before I get out of my Accord and walk toward Second Street.

The police still have the road blocked off from cars, but since I'm walking, I easily slip past the road block. Cam's former space is about halfway down the road. The mechanic where the Townsends picked up their car is nearest Main Street on the opposite side. They must have driven the car out of the shop and down Second Street. They were probably avoiding the traffic lights on Main Street since they were in a hurry to get to the school where they both worked.

The car is still sticking out of the side of the building where Cam's old kitchen used to be. It's completely smashed in, making me wonder how fast William Townsend was driving down the side street. Maybe the meeting was disciplinary in some nature, and one of them was in jeopardy of losing their job. That would certainly cause them to be stressed out and in a hurry. Cynthia said they were down one car, so money must have been tight to begin with. That would soon become much worse if one of them was about to lose their job on top of it.

I walk up to the car, which is a small blue Honda Civic. From the looks of it, they had to remove the bodies from the back of the car. The front end and both front doors are smashed so much there's no way they'd get the bodies out the front.

Without knowing why, I reach for the back door on the driver's side and open it. The smell of cappuccino hits me immediately. I'm sure the drinks spilled everywhere in the collision. Even the upholstery on the back seat has coffee stains on it. For a moment, I consider if Will was drinking his coffee and spilled it on himself while driving. That might have distracted him enough to not see the flooding on the road and lose control of the car.

I shake the thought from my mind. Even if that was what happened, it wouldn't be my fault. I only sell coffee. I have no control over what happens after that coffee leaves my shop. Still, I find myself climbing into the back seat of the car and pulling down the armrest in the center of the back seat, hoping there's a trunk access there. There is, and it's unlocked. I release the latch and pull it down, opening the small space to the trunk, which seems pretty full. I use the flashlight on my phone to better see what's inside the dark space.

"What the hell do you think you're doing?" Quentin pulls me from the car. "Jo, this is a crime scene you're tampering with."

"I think those are suitcases in the trunk," I say.

"So?"

"So, the Townsends weren't going to work. They were leaving town."

"You don't know that. Maybe they were leaving on a vacation after work, and that's why they were in such a hurry. You know what it's like trying to get ready for a vacation. There's always so much to do."

"But you'll look into it, right? See if they had travel plans?"

He shuts the car door. "Jo, let me make myself crystal clear. This accident was not caused by suitcases in the trunk. Maybe they were going on vacation and they were stressed about it. Maybe that's why Will Townsend was driving faster than he should have been given the condition of this road. It doesn't matter. The end result is still the same. Now go home, and do not let me catch you here again, or I will bring you to the station in handcuffs. Do you understand me?"

I meet his gaze. "Yeah, I understand you're not the detective I thought you were." I turn and walk back toward Main Street.

"I mean it, Jo. Stay away from this. Just because you saw them this morning doesn't mean you have a right to be involved in this."

"Funny because last time I saw a victim right before they died, you accused me of murder."

"Would you like me to do that again?" he calls after me.

"I'd like you to do your job," I say before turning onto Main Street and walking to my car, more determined than ever to find out what was really going on with Cynthia and William Townsend that led to that accident.

CHAPTER THREE

Mo, Cam, and my neighbor Jamar are all standing at my apartment door when I get there. Cam's look is more than a little disapproving. "Tell me how I managed to beat you here when you left before I did."

I unlock the door and let them all inside. Midnight goes rushing out of my apartment, nearly scaring me half to death. She's the resident black cat in the apartment complex, which used to be an old resort. Midnight hops from one apartment to the next, looking for food and good places to take naps.

"I had no idea I locked her inside when I left this morning. The poor cat." At least I had a bowl of water and some food out for her. I tend to keep the bowls full for when she wanders in, since I, like all the tenants, leave my door open when I'm home. That way Midnight can come and go as she pleases.

"You better hope she didn't poop on your pillow," Mo says. "Cats do those things when they're angry."

"Ew," I say. "Will you go check while I start dinner?"

Mo nods and heads for my bedroom.

I preheat the oven and wash my hands so I can get started on the calzone.

"So, how did I beat you here?" Cam asks me.

"I sort of went to check out the site of the accident."

"You mean the one on Second Street?" Jamar asks. "I heard about that."

"Yeah." I start working the dough onto the baking pan.

"Jo, it was an accident. Why would you go see it?" Cam asks, getting the other ingredients out of the refrigerator for me.

I shrug. "You were upset about the place, and I guess I needed to see how bad it was."

"You're in luck," Mo says. "No poop on the pillow. There was a hairball on your bathroom floor, though. I cleaned it up."

"Thanks, and I hear you owe me twenty bucks since Cam didn't charge you for your lunch," I say, giving her some major side-eye.

"I did, but then I cleaned the hairball off your bathroom floor, and we all know the going rate for that is twenty bucks, so we're even."

I shake my head, and Jamar laughs.

"I like you," he tells Mo, which makes her smile.

As I finish prepping the calzone for the oven, Cam

continues to interrogate me. "Did you find anything at the scene of the accident?"

"A lot of water in the street. Quentin was right about the drainage system not working correctly."

"Anything else?"

"Yeah, the Townsends had a trunk full of suitcases."

"Were they going away?" Cam asks.

"I think so. Quentin didn't seem to think it was a big deal, but—"

"Quentin was there?" Cam asks, leaning back against the counter.

"He sort of caught me inside the car."

"Inside?" Cam rubs the back of his neck. "Jo, what were you doing?"

I give him a recap of my encounter with Cynthia Townsend this morning. "How can I not be suspicious after that?" I ask as I put the calzone in the oven and set the timer.

"I'm with Jo," Mo says. "That does seem really odd." The second Cam and I started talking about this, she and Jamar took seats at the bar top to listen in on the conversation. At first, it annoyed me, but they both agree with me, so there's that.

"Maybe it was just prevacation jitters," Cam says.

"Now you sound like Quentin." I open a bottle of Pinot Grigio Jamar brought and grab four glasses from the cabinet.

Cam places his hand on top of mine. "Please don't

ever say that again. He's the last person I want to be compared to."

"Sorry." I know how much he dislikes Quentin.

"Are you going to look into this on your own since the police seem convinced the accident was nothing more than an accident?" Mo asks. "I mean, do you really think someone or something is to blame?"

"All I know is Cynthia looked almost scared, and if I don't try to find out why, no one else is going to." I finish pouring the wine and give everyone a glass. I raise mine. "To Cam's Kitchen. May this be the start of a successful future." I smile at Cam, and he clinks his glass against mine.

"I'll second that," Mo says before clinking her glass with Jamar's.

"What's your plan from here?" Jamar asks me. "How do you investigate without help from the police or without getting yourself arrested for tampering with an investigation?"

"It doesn't sound like there's going to be an investigation to tamper with," Mo says.

"I need to go to the high school and see if anyone there knew about Cynthia and Will's vacation. They must have put in a request for the time off."

"Good point," Mo says, "but the school closes long before you get off work."

"I know. I might have to close shop for a little while in the afternoon." I look to Cam. "I can put a sign on the door that people should go to Cam's Kitchen until I get back."

"I don't serve coffee," he says.

"I can set you up with a big urn of it. Nothing fancy, but it's caffeine."

"Or I can cover your coffee shop in the afternoon when I'm finished working at the gym," Jamar says.

I narrow my eyes at him. "You know how to make coffee? I'm talking about macchiatos, lattes, frappes, espressos..." I wave my hand, indicating the list continues.

"Can I YouTube it? Or could the daily special be black coffee?" he says, and I think he's only partially joking, but considering I just suggested bringing an urn of black coffee to Cam's Kitchen, I can see why he'd say that.

"I don't know. Maybe leaving an urn with Cam is the way to go."

"But I think I could do it. I mean, maybe a limited menu. All flavored coffees, nothing fancy."

"I suppose I could push the regular coffee with the chocolate sticks in them. Free chocolate stick with every regular coffee, including all flavored coffees." I think it over for a moment, and Jamar looks so hopeful I hate to say no. "Okay, but only if you really think you can handle it."

"Totally, and you don't even have to pay me. With all you've done for Lance, I feel like I owe you one."

"I would have helped Lance even if he wasn't your

friend. How about free coffee for a month in return?" I ask.

He extends his hand to me. "Deal."

We shake on it just as the timer on the oven goes off. "Dinner's ready."

Jamar shows up at Cup of Jo at 12:30, right on time. I decided to push the assorted flavored coffees with free chocolate sticks all day long so there isn't a major shift when I leave and Jamar covers for me. So far, people seem to be liking it. As soon as you say "free," people don't question you.

Since I have some time before the teachers leave school for the day, I give Jamar a walk-through on the shop, including a tutorial on how to use the register.

"I've filled in at the desk in the gym, so I've used a register before. This one is different, but I think I can handle it."

"I wrote down instructions for you just in case you get stuck, but you can always call me, too. I really appreciate you doing this for me."

"No problem. Thanks for trusting me. It's good to have other things to put on my resumé. You never know what will happen in the future."

"Are you looking to do something other than being a personal trainer?"

"Not right now, but we'll see what happens. I let my

boss know I was working another job today. It's been a while since I got a raise. Let him think I have something better lined up."

I laugh. "I see. Well, don't let him know I'm paying you in coffee, then, or your plan might backfire."

"Good point."

A customer comes to the counter, and I let Jamar take care of them. I stand nearby in case he needs help but let him figure things out for himself. He presses the wrong button on the register, but he realizes his mistake and clears out the sale before trying again. He gets it on his second attempt.

"Nice work." I grab my jacket and purse from under the counter. "I should be back in an hour or so."

"No problem. I've got this." He waves to me as I leave.

I walk by Cam's Kitchen and peek inside. He has two customers at a table, eating lunch. Considering he makes baked goods, his bigger crowd comes in the morning for the Danishes, donuts, and muffins, or in the afternoon for snacks like cupcakes, brownies, and cookies. I quickly go inside to say hello to him.

"Heading to the school?" he asks me.

"Yeah. Jamar seems to be okay over there."

"I'll peek in on him in a few to make sure."

"Thanks, but don't leave your customers unattended. I'm sure he'll be fine."

"Keep me posted with what you find out," he says.

"Will do." I give him a smile before leaving. I hate to

give up my parking spot on the busy Main Street, but I don't want to walk the two miles to the school because it would take me longer to get back and relieve Jamar. I drive to the school and have to go through the process of being buzzed inside and then checked in through security. Since I don't have an appointment, I have to sit outside the main office and wait until someone can see me. I keep checking my watch.

A few kids walk down the hallway in my direction, and even though I know I shouldn't ask them questions, I find myself blurting out, "Excuse me."

The two girls stop and look at me.

"Hi, I was curious if either of you are students of Mr. or Mrs. Townsend."

"I have Mr. Townsend for biology," the taller of the two girls says. "Or I guess I should say I did."

I'm not surprised they've heard about the accident. News travels quickly in this town. "Yes, I'm so sorry to hear about the accident. And to think he and his wife were about to leave for vacation, too." I'm hoping one of them talked about the vacation in class.

"That sucks," the shorter girl says.

"Yeah, I wonder where they were going," the other girl adds.

"Oh, he didn't mention it to you guys? Didn't mention how long he planned to be away?" I ask.

The girl shakes her head. "He's not a big talker. Not when it comes to socializing with his students at least. He can lecture about biology until you pass out, though."

She stops talking when her friend gives her a look. "Sorry. I shouldn't talk about him like that after what happened."

A woman steps out of the office. "Ms. Coffee?"

"Yes." I jump to my feet, and the two girls continue on their way.

The woman holds the door open for me. "Come inside."

The nameplate on her desk reads "Susan Bell." "Thank you for seeing me, Ms. Bell." I take a seat on the opposite side of her desk.

"Oh, I'm not Ms. Bell. She's out today. I'm her secretary, Katrina Davis." She sits down.

"I see. Well, I was just trying to find out if Cynthia and William Townsend had taken vacation days for this week."

"And you are?"

I have no justifiable reason for her to give me this information. I can't mention the Bennett Falls Police Department, or I'll have Quentin pounding down my door, possibly with handcuffs at the ready. "I was a friend of Cynthia's," I say. "I know I shouldn't be asking, but Cynthia was so upset yesterday morning, and I can't help feeling like something was wrong." Most of that is true, so I don't feel like I'm completely deceiving the woman.

"Wrong in what way?"

"Well, she was in an awful hurry to get to work for that meeting."

"What meeting was that?" she asks.

"Oh, I'm not sure who it was with. I'd guess maybe the principal, though."

She shakes her head. "No, I work for the principal as well as for Ms. Bell. He didn't have a meeting with Cynthia scheduled for yesterday."

"He didn't? What about with William Townsend?"

"No. Not with him either."

Then I must be right. They weren't coming to the school at all. "Do you know where they were planning to go on their vacation? I assume that was the cause of whatever was bringing them in early yesterday."

"No, but hang on." She types something into the computer on Susan Bell's desk. "There's nothing in the system about either of them taking vacation days."

The school had no idea Cynthia and William were leaving town. Something was definitely going on with them. "Have they missed a lot of school days before?"

"Look, Ms. Coffee, I really can't give you that kind of information. I've said too much as it is. I could get in serious trouble for this."

I stand up. "Well, I certainly don't want to get you into any trouble. Thank you very much for your time, Ms. Davis."

"Mrs.," she says, holding up her left hand. "Got married two months ago."

"Oh, well, congratulations. I appreciate you speaking with me since Mrs. Bell is out."

"She's a Ms. She's not married."

I nod. "Thank you again." I walk back to the man at

the security desk and sign out. Hopefully, Quentin won't show up here and see my name on the sign-in sheet, but seeing as he didn't think this was worth looking into, I doubt he'll come here to ask questions.

I leave the school and drive back to Cup of Jo. The place is swarming with customers. To the point where I worry I'll get in trouble by the fire department for having too many people inside the shop. Once I get into the place, I see why. Jamar is putting on a show while serving the coffees. He's dancing, singing, and twirling all around the floor.

"Oh, hey, Jo," he says when he sees me. "Everything's great. People have been coming in nonstop."

"I think they're enjoying the entertainment," I say, removing my jacket and storing it and my purse under the counter.

"Sorry. I just sort of got carried away."

"No need to apologize. It looks like you raked in quite a bit of business." Even the tip mug is overflowing. I take the money from inside it—minus the ten-dollar bill Cam gave me for good luck when I opened Cup of Jo, which I have taped inside—and hand it to Jamar. "Here. This is yours."

"No, I couldn't." He holds up both hands.

"Jamar, the customers tip their servers. You were their server. It's yours." I push the money toward him.

"Are you sure?" he asks. "This looks like a lot."

"I agree. It does, and yes, it's yours."

"This is awesome. Thank you, Jo. Anytime you need

someone to cover the shop, let me know. I'm your man."
He grabs his jacket and starts for the door.

An idea hits me instantly. "Jamar," I call after him.
"How would you like a job?"

He stops and turns back to me. "Wait. Are you serious?"

I nod. "Very."

"You'd have to teach me to make the other drinks."

"I'm willing to teach you if you're willing to learn," I say.

His eyes widen. "You're really serious?"

"One hundred percent."

"When should I start?" he asks with a huge smile.

The door behind Jamar opens, and Quentin walks in looking extremely unhappy.

"How about right now?" I ask.

Jamar retakes his spot behind the counter. "Who's next?" he asks, and when a woman walks up to the counter, he spins and dips her before taking her order. I almost laugh, but Quentin takes my arm and pulls me outside.

"We need to have a chat, and you'd better be able to convince me you had a great reason for questioning people at the high school, or so help me, Jo, I will slap handcuffs on you."

There goes my good mood.

CHAPTER FOUR

I wrap my arms around myself since my jacket is inside Cup of Jo. "Can we talk inside? It's cold out here."

Quentin looks around me. "I'm not sure you can fit anyone else in there. You might be breaking the fire code as it is."

"Jamar started working for me. He's quite the crowd pleaser." I rub my arms, trying to warm up.

The door to Cam's Kitchen opens, and Cam walks out, holding his coat, which he immediately gives to me. "What's going on?"

"This doesn't concern you, Cam," Quentin says.

"Anything you have to say to me, you can say in front of Cam. I'm just going to tell him about it anyway," I say.

Quentin's jaw clenches. "Fine. Jo, you can't go asking questions at the high school like that. You're not part of this investigation."

"Is there an investigation?" I ask. "Because last time we spoke, you were convinced this was an accident. Yet no one at the school knew Cynthia and William were leaving town. They didn't take vacation days. Something was going on. There's a reason why Cynthia was looking over her shoulder, and despite your fiancée thinking it was because Will was outside, that's not what it was. They were running from something."

Quentin rubs his forehead. "Okay, first, I disagree, but I did follow up and call the school. They confirmed that Cynthia and William hadn't requested time off. But..." He holds up a hand to keep me from protesting. "There's a good chance that's what the early meeting was about."

"The meeting no one in the office knew anything about? I talked to the principal's secretary. She said neither had a meeting with the principal."

"Are you denying the flooded street is the most likely cause of the accident?" Quentin asks me. "You saw it for yourself."

"I did, and maybe that's what caused the car to go out of control, but there was another reason why William Townsend was speeding."

"What makes you think he was?" Quentin asks me.

"I can't prove he was, but the police can, right? Can't you guys figure out how fast he must have been traveling at the time of the crash?" I've watched enough crime shows to know that's how it's done. Of course, it's hard to know what's real and what's altered to make a show more dramatic and interesting.

"We can, and we will."

"You really are looking into this," I say. "Since when?"

Quentin huffs. "Since last night when…" His gaze goes to Cam, and I know he doesn't want to voice the fact that he caught me at the scene of the accident going through the Townsends' car. Even though Cam wouldn't tell anyone, we're out on the street where other people can overhear us. "Just do me a favor and please stay away from this." The look in his eyes says so much more than his words do.

"You think I'm right. You don't want me to be right, but you think I might be. That's why you called the school."

"I admit the suitcases raised some questions, but *I* will find out what was going on. Not you, Jo." He motions to Cup of Jo. "Run your coffee shop. Let me do my job."

I nod, not because I'm agreeing to back off, but because I'm agreeing to let him investigate the case, which is what I wanted from the start.

He turns and walks away.

"Why do I feel like you two spend more time together now than you did when you were dating?" Cam asks.

"It unfortunately feels that way to me, too." I remove Cam's coat. "Thank you for the jacket. Quentin would have let me freeze to death out here."

"You should get back inside and have a nice warm coffee."

"I'd rather hang out at Cam's Kitchen if that's okay with you. Jamar has my place covered." I hitch my thumb over my shoulder, where Jamar is dancing and swinging a dish towel over his head. "Should I worry he's going to start dancing on tables?"

Cam puts his arm around my shoulders. "Nah. He'll behave. Besides, the crowd loves him." He opens the door to Cam's Kitchen, and the warmth that greets me is so inviting.

I sit down at an empty table near the display case. "What do you recommend today, Mr. Turner?" I ask.

He goes behind the counter and pulls a pecan pie from the case. "How about some pecan pie? You can forgo the scoop of vanilla ice cream on top if you're too cold."

"Forgo the ice cream? That's just crazy talk. Bring it on. I'll go get us some coffee from next door." I stand up, but Mo comes walking into Cam's Kitchen holding a drink caddy with three large coffees.

"Jamar is a hoot! Seriously! The older ladies are loving him." She places the drink caddy on the table. "I saw you come in here after you talked to Quentin."

From her office across the street, Mo's view of my coffee shop couldn't be better, so I have no doubt she saw the whole thing.

"You looked like you were freezing out there when Mr. Ice in His Veins decided to interrogate you in the cold," she says. "That is until Cam brought you his jacket."

Cam brings two slices of pecan pie with ice cream and sets them in front of us before going to get one for himself.

I take a coffee and sniff it before sipping it. "Hazelnut, my favorite."

"Of course. You've even got me hooked on it."

Cam returns with his slice of pie and sits down. "Jo got Quentin to look into the accident."

"Why am I not surprised? He's totally afraid of you showing him up. Again, if I might add."

I'm not entirely sure I solved the last case on my own. I sort of unknowingly got someone to confess to more than I thought they actually did. It all worked out in the end, though.

I fill them both in on what I learned at the school. "It seems like they were running from something, right?" I ask once I'm finished talking.

"It could be. I wish I'd seen Cynthia in Cup of Jo yesterday so I could back you up on her behavior, but my view inside the shop isn't good. I did see Will on the sidewalk, though."

"What did he seem like?" I ask, taking a bite of pie since Cam and Mo are already finished and I've barely eaten.

"He was on his phone, but he kept glancing up and down the street. I thought he was waiting for a ride at first, but you told me he was picking up his car from the mechanic."

"A lot of people get their cars checked out before they go on a long trip, so that could support your theory that they were running away," Cam says. "Maybe the story about the brakes was to throw people off."

"I guess it could have been. Cup of Jo has become a hotspot for local gossip, unfortunately. If Cynthia and Will wanted to start a rumor, it makes sense they'd do it at my coffee shop."

"What do you mean unfortunately?" Mo asks. "You've totally gotten more business thanks to that."

"True, although with Jamar working for me, I don't think I'll need to worry about business."

"Cam, you should get Jamar to work here, too," Mo says, looking around at the empty bakery.

"I was afraid of this happening. People in town already had places where they bought their baked goods, and I was making good money supplying those places. Now…" He sighs.

I put my hand on top of his. "Don't give up. It's only been two days. Once people realize the only place to get your baked goods now is here, they'll be flocking to your door." I hope. If I derailed Cam's career, I'll never forgive myself.

"I agree with Jo. Things will pick up. But maybe you should advertise more," Mo says. "I can help you. I take payment in pie."

"Done," Cam says.

"I'll have more time after Friday. Lance is pretty much set up for his grand opening."

"Speaking of, we're all still going, right?" Cam asks.

"Yeah, us, Jamar, and a bunch of his other friends," I say.

"Unless you two want it to be a date," Mo says. "I don't want to intrude. If Jamar is going with other friends, that makes me the third wheel with you guys."

"Don't be silly," Cam says. "This has been planned for a month. Besides, Jo and I can go on dates any time we want." He smiles at me.

"Okay. I'll try to find a date, though. Just so I don't feel weird."

"What about Lance?" I ask. "I sort of thought he had a thing for you when you two met."

"Lance? Really? He's a really sweet guy, but I don't know. There's this new guy at my office. He's cute. Like so cute I actually giggled when he said hi to me the day we met." She waves a hand in the air. "It was so awkward, and I'm still embarrassed, but maybe I can just tell him a friend and client of mine owns the restaurant and I'm trying to get more people there for the opening."

"Go for it," I tell her because I can't imagine this guy, no matter how cute he is, saying no to dinner with Mo. She's beautiful and funny, and people who aren't related to her rarely want to slap her. Well, maybe Quentin, but he deserves her snark.

"Okay, I'll do it. Just be prepared to console me with lots of pie if he says no." She points her fork at Cam.

"I'll have plenty ready just in case, but I don't think you'll need it." He grabs our empty plates and clears them.

Mo finishes her coffee before asking, "Where is your investigation taking you next?"

"Well, I wish I could check out their house, but I can't because I don't have a warrant or a badge, and they also lived alone so there's no one to let me in. I can't check their credit cards either to see if they booked a trip. Really, all I can do is talk to people and see who knew of their plans. If anyone did."

"They must have had people they talked to at work, right? I mean the teachers' lounge is probably a great spot for people to talk about upcoming plans. Someone had to know."

"And how exactly do I get inside the teacher's lounge?"

"Pose as a teacher?"

"You mean substitute teach? No way. Not happening. Besides, I'd have to go through the approval process, and there's no time for that."

"Okay, then I'll check out her social media profiles and see which of her friends there also work at the high school," Mo says, already on her phone.

I scoot closer to get a better view of her phone. "Erica Daniels. I know her," I say. "She lives in my apartment complex. Second floor, I believe."

"Want me to go with you to talk to her later?" Cam says, wiping down the table.

I look at the clock on the wall. School should be over for the day, and I don't want to sit around until it's time for him to close. "I'll go on ahead. She might give me a lead that you can help me follow up on later."

He nods. "All right. Keep me posted."

I will. I stand up. "Thanks, Mo. Are you joining Cam and me for dinner tonight?"

"No, I'm going to stay a little late at work to finish up some things for Lance."

"And maybe talk to that cute new guy?" I ask.

She bobs one shoulder. "We'll see. It's his first week, so he's been staying late to impress the boss. It's possible we'll be the only two people in the office." She gives me a sly smile.

"Good luck," I tell her, and she gets up to leave.

I look at Cam, who is staring at the wall connecting his bakery to Cup of Jo. The laughter coming through the wall is proof that Jamar is still entertaining a large crowd. "It's funny how he's able to get so many people in there when I never could."

Cam turns to me and smiles. "I know you're just trying to make me feel better, and I appreciate it, but your coffee shop was successful before Jamar ever stepped foot in it."

"Maybe, but this place will be successful as well. I guarantee it."

"I guess it's just you and me for dinner tonight," he says.

"That all depends on what I learn from Erica

42

Daniels. It might be you, me, and someone who knows more about what was really going on with Cynthia and William Townsend."

Before heading to Erica's apartment, I stop in Cup of Jo and ask Jamar to recommend Cam's Kitchen to the customers before they leave. He agrees since he loves Cam's baking. Hopefully, it helps.

Erica answers her door in yoga pants and a loose-fitting crew neck sweatshirt that hangs off one shoulder. "Jo, nice to see you."

"Hi, Erica. I was hoping you had a minute."

"Sure. I was just doing some yoga, but I paused it. Come in." She steps aside to allow me to enter. Her apartment is identical to mine, and she has the couch pushed back against the wall and a yoga mat in the center of the floor. "Can I get you something to drink? I just made cucumber water."

"No, I'm fine, thanks. I was hoping you could tell me if Cynthia Townsend had any vacation plans."

"Not that she mentioned to me, and I really doubt she'd be able to afford it."

"Because of the car situation?" I ask.

"You know about that?" She sits down on the yoga mat and motions toward the couch.

I sit down. "She told me her car died and Will's was getting new brakes."

"Yeah, it was rotten timing with the house thing and all." She extends her legs in front of her and leans forward, placing her head on her knees.

"What was going on with the house?" I ask.

"The landlord was kicking them out. They missed a few months' rent because Cynthia's mom was in the hospital and Cynthia and Will got stuck paying the bills since her mom doesn't have health insurance. It was a bad situation. The landlord let them slide for three months, but after that, he said he couldn't afford to let them keep living there."

Were the suitcases in the trunk because they were leaving town or because they had to pack up all their stuff and get out of the house? They might have been living out of the car. "That's awful. What's going to happen to Cynthia's mom now?"

"Oh, she's out of the hospital and doing much better. I'm assuming Cynthia's sister will have to fly out from California if she needs any additional care or money." Erica presses the bottoms of her feet together with her knees bent outward.

"That explains why Cynthia was so jittery Monday morning. I feel awful she was dealing with so much."

"Yeah, and then that accident happened. It's terrible. Her students are really upset."

"I can imagine."

"Between Cynthia and Will, they knew just about everyone at the school. Even some of the staff is taking it very hard. A few people took off yesterday and today because coming in is too difficult for them right now."

I remember a teacher passed away when I was in high school. We had grief counsellors, and substitute teachers covered most of the classes since the teacher who died was friends with quite a few of his colleagues. "Schools tend to be close-knit environments," I say.

She nods.

"Was there anyone in particular that either was close to?" I ask.

"I didn't know Will very well. The science wing is sort of its own entity. I teach art, so Cynthia and I had classrooms in neighboring hallways since the music and art wings are near each other. Cynthia was friends with just about everyone, though."

"Well, I'm very sorry for your loss," I tell Erica.

"Thank you. Same to you."

I don't bother to tell her I wasn't really friends with Cynthia or Will. People will wonder why I'm asking so many questions if I admit to that. I just nod politely and stand up. The school might be a dead end, but I can follow up with the landlord about the rent and at least see if they had plans to move or if they were living out of their car. And if they were living out of their car, where were they staying Sunday night? That could play a key role in what happened Monday morning to cause the accident.

CHAPTER FIVE

Cam and I are just finishing dinner at an Irish Pub near the house Cynthia and William Townsend rented when my phone chimes with a text from Mo. I had her look up who their landlord was and where he lives so we can pay him a visit.

"I've got a name and address," I tell Cam.

He finishes the last bite of his Reuben and takes a sip of iced tea before asking, "Is it nearby?"

"Rudy Wilcox lives on the same road as the house he rents. Talk about Big Brother is watching. I mean, according to Erica, he let the Townsends slide on the rent for a little while, but I can't imagine it was comfortable seeing each other on a regular basis with that much money being owed."

"That could be why Cynthia was looking over her shoulder," Cam says. "It could be a conditioned response to always look out for the landlord because she didn't have the money to pay rent."

"I guess, but they were already out of the house by Monday morning, so why would Cynthia care if Rudy was around?"

"I doubt he just let the owed rent go. They probably worked out a payment plan or something," Cam says.

"Maybe." I eat another French fry as I consider it.

"You're not happy with that explanation, though."

"Not really. No."

"Does that mean you suspect Rudy Wilcox of doing something to them?"

"What if they were leaving town and he knew it? He might have thought they weren't going to pay him what he's owed."

"And you think he might have gone after them to try to get the money before they left." Cam nods and takes another sip of iced tea. "That's possible. I doubt he'll admit that to us, though."

"No. But we can find out what kind of car he drives and see if anyone remembers seeing it on Main Street Monday morning. If someone does, it might mean he was there and watching the Townsends."

"That would explain a lot. Though I don't think it changes the fact that the accident was an accident after all."

"Is it weird that I don't think it was?" I ask as the waiter brings the bill to the table. I reach for it, but Cam quickly snatches it up. "I invited you along tonight. It's my treat," I say, holding out my hand.

He removes his credit card from his wallet and hands it to the waiter. Once the waiter leaves, Cam meets my gaze. "I know you're worried about my money situation thanks to the bakery opening not going well, but I'm fine."

I want to tell him that's not what it is, but we'd both know I was lying. "Just so you know, the two of us dating does not mean you get to pay for everything."

"I don't pay for everything. Most nights, you make me dinner at your apartment. You pay for all the food on those occasions."

I didn't think about that. "Touché, Mr. Turner," I say before finishing my iced tea.

The waiter returns with Cam's card, and after signing the bill, we're ready to go see Rudy Wilcox. I put the address into my phone's navigation, even though I'm familiar with the road he lives on. It's mostly so I don't get lost in my thoughts about the case and forget to tell Cam where to go.

"Can I ask you what it is about this case that makes you think there's more to it?" Cam asks, making the turn my phone just directed him to.

"A feeling mostly. But I think it's the fact that the police were so sure this was nothing more than a car accident. They weren't going to look into it."

"But Quentin is now, right?"

"He is, but who knows how many other cases he's

also working. He might not have much time to put into this one. Plus, being the last one to see Cynthia, I feel a little obligated to find out what happened to her."

Cam reaches over and squeezes my hand. "There is no one else quite like you, Jo Coffee."

We pull up to Rudy Wilcox's house, and since his car is in the driveway, I have high hopes we'll get some answers from him. Cam knocks on the door, and it only takes a moment before we hear Rudy yell, "Just a minute." I can hear a strange thumping sound as his footsteps get closer.

Rudy answers the door in his bathrobe and holding a cane in his left hand. "Can I help you?"

"Are you Rudy Wilcox?" I ask.

"That's me."

"Hi, I'm Joanna Coffee, and this is Camden Turner."

"Coffee. You own the coffee shop on Main Street, right?"

"That's correct," I say.

"You deliver?" he jokes. "I don't see any coffee on you."

"No, sorry, I don't. We were actually hoping to ask you a few questions about the Townsends."

"Oh." His tone is unreadable. Is he upset because they're dead or upset because their death means he'll never get his money?

"We know they owed you several months' rent because of Cynthia's mother's medical bills."

He nods. "I tried to help them out, but I have to earn

a living, too." He raises his cane a few inches off the ground and quickly puts it back down. "I have a bad leg. I can't really do much to make money, so that house is my source of income. I couldn't let them stay there any longer for free." He looks down. "You probably think I'm awful for putting them out."

"No, Cam and I own our own businesses. We understand what it's like. You have to pay your bills just like everyone else."

"Will got really angry. He started cursing at me. Told me I'm the lowest form of scum there is for tossing them out on the street." Rudy leans against the doorframe and meets Cam's gaze. "I was actually going to your grand opening on Monday morning, but I saw Will standing on the sidewalk in front of your place. I couldn't face him, so I just drove on by."

"Did Will see you?" I ask.

"Yeah, he did. He knows my car, and I swear he looked straight through the car window at me. You know that feeling when you sense someone shooting you death glares."

If Will did see Rudy, he might have been so angry that he'd go speeding out of the mechanic's to try to leave town and put all this behind him.

"Mr. Wilcox, when did the Townsends leave the home they were renting from you?" Cam asks.

"A couple days ago."

"Were they living out of their car by any chance?" I ask.

"Beats me. I know her car died, though. They had to have it towed away."

Which I doubt they could afford, but what about the twenty-dollar bill Cynthia gave me? She was throwing around money like someone who wasn't in debt. Yet that doesn't go along with what I've learned about her.

"Do you know if they had plans to leave town?" I ask.

Rudy shrugs. "They didn't talk to me after Will blew up in my face. I tried to make him understand my situation, but he didn't want to hear it. He told me to rot in hell, and he packed up the car and left. I'm afraid that's all I can tell you."

"Thank you for your time, Mr. Wilcox," Cam says.

We turn to leave when Rudy says, "Oh, there is one more thing. Before Will screamed at me, I slipped a couple twenties under their front door. To show them I felt bad for the way things happened." He lowers his gaze to the floor. "I'm not a heartless man."

I step up to him and place my hand on his shoulder. "I know you're not. That was very thoughtful of you. Thank you again for speaking with us."

Rudy nods and closes the door.

"That explains why Cynthia had that twenty-dollar bill to pay me with," I say as we get back in the car.

Cam turns on the heat. It's not a particularly cold evening, but considering Rudy never invited us in, we were talking outside for several minutes. "Where to?" Cam asks me.

"Home, I guess. We have no idea where the Townsends spent the night after dropping off the car at the mechanic's, and the shop is closed for the day, so we can't talk to the mechanic who worked on the car either."

"Home it is." Cam pulls out of the driveway and onto the road. "Why do you think he didn't invite us in?"

"Easy. He has trouble getting around. I'm willing to bet his house isn't in any shape to entertain guests."

"I feel like you believe him and don't think he had anything to do with the accident."

"Yes, I believe him, but the fact that Rudy was there and Will most likely saw him could have sent Will into a rage that caused him to drive like a maniac."

"Which would mean it was just an accident," Cam says.

"Are you trying to tell me I'm wasting my time looking into this?" I ask.

"No, of course not, it's just that everything is pointing to what the police already believe."

I lower my head. "I know it is, but I just can't believe that's really what happened. Cynthia was scared of something, and she wound up dying moments later."

"Then let's keep looking into it," Cam says, giving my hand another squeeze.

He drives me home and stops at the door instead of coming inside. "I'm beat. I never knew not being busy could be so exhausting. The only good part about it is I'm able to donate a lot of food to the local shelter at the end of the day. I'm helping people that way."

"Cam, I'm so sorry."

"It's okay. And I know you asked Jamar to send people my way. He did, too. This one little girl wanted a cupcake, and after her mother bought one, I gave her eleven more to make it an even dozen."

The worst part is that because Cam severed ties with the businesses he used to bake for, none of them will be willing to take him back if he asks. I have a feeling some of those business owners might be telling people not to buy from Cam's Kitchen as a result. And I plan to find out for sure.

I cup Cam's cheek. "It's going to get better. Please don't give up yet."

"Good night, Jo." He leans down to give me a quick kiss, and then he walks toward the elevator.

I open my door and step inside, leaving the door open behind me. I hear Midnight's meow as she comes running in.

"She's excited to see you," Jamar says, following behind Midnight. "She was at my place."

"Hey, thanks again for all your help today."

"Are you kidding me? I've never had so much fun and gotten paid to do it."

"I'm glad. I'll be honest, after I asked if you wanted a job, I questioned if I'd be able to pay you, but with the amount of people you're bringing in and the sales you're making, we'll both be paid well."

"How's Cam's place doing?" he asks, opening my refrigerator and grabbing a bottle of water.

"Not well. Thanks for trying to get people over there for him."

Jamar takes a long swig of water. "You know, some people scoffed when I mentioned going to Cam's Kitchen. It was a little strange."

"I was thinking someone might be trying to sabotage his new business."

"You might be right." He takes another drink of water. "Any idea who?"

"I'm going to ask around to find out, but it must be one of the people he used to supply baked goods for, don't you think?"

"I'll see what I can find out tomorrow. You still want me to work the afternoon shift after I'm finished at the gym, right?"

"Yeah, as long as you're up for it."

"Great. I'll just shower, eat, and head over when I'm done." He points a finger at me. "Hey, do you think Cam would want to provide desserts for Lance? I know he's looking to expand the dessert options. They'd need to be fancy, though. I don't know if that's Cam's thing."

"You should have Lance call Cam. I don't think he'd turn him down."

Jamar nods. "I'll do that. See you tomorrow, Boss."

Wednesday morning, I'm just opening up shop when Quentin walks in.

"What are you doing here?" I ask him. "Did I do something else that you want to admonish me for?"

"No, I wanted to let you know I followed up with the investigation of the car. It turns out there was no brake fluid."

"No brake fluid? You mean Will couldn't have stopped or even slowed the car?" I ask.

Quentin shakes his head.

"But the mechanic had just fixed the brakes the day before. Will and Cynthia were on their way to pick up the car."

"I know. I'm heading there now and thought you might want to tag along."

I study Quentin's face. "You don't think the brake fluid was an accident. You think the Townsends were murdered."

"Isn't that what you're thinking, too, after hearing that?"

I nod because that's exactly what I'm thinking. Now the question is who wanted to kill them?

CHAPTER SIX

There's just one problem with Quentin's lead. I can't leave Cup of Jo, and Jamar won't be here until this afternoon. "I can't go with you now. I just opened."

"Tell you what. I have another case I'm working on. How about I pick you up after lunch?"

Cam chooses that exact moment to walk in, and I know he heard that last part and totally misunderstood it. "What's going on?"

"Quentin found out something important and wants me to tag along with the investigation," I blurt out, not wanting Cam to get the wrong idea.

"I'll be back later," Quentin says, turning and walking by Cam to leave the shop as quickly as possible.

"He really doesn't like me, does he?" Cam asks.

"For one, we both know the feeling is mutual. And Quentin also told me he always suspected there was something between you and me."

"But he's with Sam, so why would he be bitter about that?" Cam asks.

"He's Quentin. I'll never understand why he does anything."

A few customers walk in and greet us. "I'll be right with you," I tell them, not wanting to dismiss Cam.

Cam moves toward me. "I'm going to talk to the landlord. The rent for Cam's Kitchen is paid through the month, but I'm not going to lease the space beyond that."

"Cam, no. You can't give up. It's only been two days. My shop was closed down after half a day, and it took me a week to reopen. Now look at the place."

"I'm glad I tried it, but it's clear it's not going to work out. It's okay. Really. Lance called me last night anyway. He wants me to bake desserts for him."

"Why don't you sound happy about that?"

"It feels like a step backward, I guess. I shouldn't complain, though. I need the money, and this would be steady work."

"Do both. Bake for Lance's restaurant and keep your own bakery."

"You mean take a real job to fund my dream that's clearly not going to make any money?" He gives me a sad smile. "One day, I'm going to want to have a family. I don't want to be a drain on anyone else."

"But—"

"You have customers. Don't keep them waiting." He turns and walks out.

I force a smile on my face and start taking orders.

Mickey Baldwin comes in and takes his usual seat. I'm not sure what he does for a living since he always seems to be here. Maybe he's a trust fund baby. Or he secretly won the lottery. Or maybe he still lives at home with his mother. I really don't know his story.

"Hey, Jo. I need a cup of joe." Mickey laughs at his joke. "When are you going to get servers in here?" he asks. "I was on my feet all night."

I get him a cup of dark roast, knowing it's his favorite, and bring it over to him with a chocolate stick. "What is it that you do, Mickey? I've never asked."

"I'm a nighttime janitor at the high school."

"You are?" Could this be any more perfect?

"For twenty years now."

"Then I suppose you knew Cynthia and Will Townsend."

"As well as you can know anyone after cleaning up after them." He laughs, unwraps the chocolate stick, and puts it in his mug. "These new mugs?"

"Yeah, I bought them to match the tip mug Cam got for me."

"I like them. Cam's place isn't doing too well, huh?"

I sit down in the empty chair. "Any idea why that is?"

"I'm looking at her."

"Me?" I jerk my head back. "What are you talking about, Mickey?"

"Little Jo Coffee comes back after getting her heart torn in two, she gets falsely accused of poisoning the

58

richest man in town, then solves the murder herself, and donates her inheritance to a struggling local. You're our new local celebrity. The men in town don't like Cam on account of he's taken you off the market. And the women, well, you provide them with chocolate and coffee. What more do I need to say?"

"But what does that have to do with Cam's bakery? Everyone loved his baked goods when he sold them to other stores."

"And they still love them, but at the end of the day, the people in this town would rather invest their money in you."

"But Cam helped me solve that murder. I couldn't have done it without him. I couldn't have opened this place without him."

Mickey holds up both hands. "Hey, I like the guy. You don't have to convince me of anything."

"But his business is failing, Mickey." And to find out it's my fault is too much for me to handle.

"If you ask me, you two should have stayed in business together. Nobody's sabotaging him. He's just the unfortunate by-product of you being famous around here right now." Mickey points behind me. "Speaking of, you've got a line."

"Thanks, Mickey." I get up and help my customers.

When Mickey's finished with his coffee and chocolate, he comes to the counter to pay his bill and put a dollar in my tip mug.

"Thanks for talking to me about Cam," I say.

"I'm going to his place now to buy something. Maybe a pie to bring to work later."

"Speaking of work, how well did you know Cynthia and Will?" Talk about Cam earlier made me forget the real question I wanted to ask Mickey. "Did either fight with any of their colleagues?"

"Most of the teachers are gone by the time I get to the school. I do see some interesting things, though."

"Like what?"

"Cars still in the parking lot even though no one seems to be around."

"Cars? Like people are leaving them there overnight?"

"Or they're inside them out there."

"Are you suggesting things were going on in secret between some of the teachers?" I ask.

"Let's just say I've found letters and other things in garbage cans that suggest more than one of the staff members was involved in extracurricular activities, if you know what I mean."

"Was Cynthia or Will Townsend one of them?"

"I did see Cynthia's car there late a few times."

"So, she and Will have stayed late, but why?"

"Not Will. He was never there late. Only once did I see him, and he was speeding out of the parking lot, heading in the opposite direction."

I lean on the counter. "Wait. You're saying Cynthia and Will didn't drive to work together?"

"Nope. Not until her car died."

"Any idea why they wouldn't carpool when they lived and worked together?"

"I guess she liked to hang around after school, and he either had another job to get to or somewhere else he wanted to be."

They were having money troubles, so a second job would make sense. I'll have to look into that. "Thanks, Mickey. You've been really helpful."

"With what exactly? Why are you so interested in Will and Cynthia Townsend?"

I know better than to tell Mickey that the police suspect the accident was really murder. He'd tell half the town by midday. "I just realized I didn't know them very well. It's so sad what happened to them."

"Well, at least Cam can be thankful he wasn't still working out of that kitchen."

"You can say that again."

Mickey pats the counter before turning and walking away.

Samantha rushes up to the counter. "Jo, I heard you're going to help Quentin solve the murder."

Mickey turns back around to face me. "Murder? What's she talking about?"

Now every head in the shop is facing my direction.

My mind races, trying to concoct a way to turn this conversation around. I force a laugh. "That's silly, Samantha. We already solved the murder, remember?" I grab her arm and pull her to the back storage room.

"No, Quentin just told me you were going to the mechanic's place with him."

Just my luck that Quentin finally started talking to his fiancée about his cases when I want to keep this quiet. If the Townsends were murdered, someone in town killed them. It's best if everyone thinks it was only an accident. Then, someone might slip up, and we can catch them.

"Shh." I press a finger to my lips. "When Quentin tells you about cases, you can't go telling everyone."

"I'm not telling everyone. I'm telling you, and you already know. I don't see what the big deal is, Jo." She crosses her arms.

Sometimes dealing with her is like dealing with a child. I don't know how Quentin does it. I certainly can't imagine her raising children one day. I shake the thought from my mind. "Yes, I do know about it, but everyone else in the shop doesn't need to know. That's why we're talking back here right now."

"Oh, I see. Sorry about that. I'm just so upset about it all. I saw Will on the sidewalk Monday morning. He didn't look happy. Do you think he knew someone was trying to kill him?" she asks me.

"I don't know. Maybe. Cynthia was pretty spooked, so that could be the case." I can't believe I'm discussing this with her, but I really don't have anyone else I can talk to at the moment.

She latches onto my arm with both hands. "Will you promise me you'll look out for Quentin?"

Me look out for Quentin? He's the one with a gun!

"I don't want him out there chasing down murderers. What if he gets hurt? What would I do?"

That's a good question. Before Quentin, Samantha had me looking after her. She's like a lost little puppy. She needs someone who is going to take care of her. "Quentin and I will look out for each other, okay?"

She nods. "Thanks, Jo. I can always count on you."

As soon as Samantha leaves, I call Mo. "Hey, you busy? I haven't seen you today."

"Sorry. I meant to come by for my morning coffee, but I got caught up talking to Wes."

"Wes?" I ask. "Is that the new guy at work?"

"It is. We struck up a conversation yesterday, and we sort of hit it off. He came right to my office when he got here this morning so he could say hello. How sweet is that?"

"Very sweet. Why don't you bring him by on your lunch break so I can meet him?"

"Are you insane? I can't introduce him to my family yet? It's way too soon for that. I'd scare him away."

"Okay, fine, but how are you surviving without coffee?"

"I asked one of the interns to get my coffee for me. You served him. Young kid, about twenty. Red hair. Lots of freckles."

"I think I remember him. Hey, I need you to do some internet magic and find out if William Townsend was working a second job."

"Okay, I'll try, but I'm not sure I'll be able to come up

with an answer for you. What makes you suspect he was, anyway?"

"Mickey Baldwin is a night janitor at the high school."

"Oh, yeah. I knew that."

"He said he thought Will might have been working another job because he went speeding out of the parking lot at the end of the day."

"Could just mean he liked to drive fast. That *is* what caused the accident."

"Not necessarily. According to Quentin, the evaluation of the car revealed there was no brake fluid. It's possible someone tampered with the car."

"Then it was murder?" she practically shrieks.

I hear someone in the background but can't make out what they're saying.

"Oh, hi, Wes. Yeah, can you believe someone murdered Will and Cynthia Townsend? Crazy, right? I mean—"

"Mo!" I yell into the phone.

"Ow! My ear, Jo."

"Sorry, but that was confidential information."

"Oh. Sorry. Um, I should go. I'll talk to you soon." She hangs up.

I'm tempted to go to the window to see if she's going somewhere with Wes, but I'm already positive she is. I hope she thinks to bring him to Cam's Kitchen. He might not have coffee to go with his baked goods, but he does sell bottled drinks in there. It's crazy how the products we sell go so well together yet we have two completely separate shops. I need to talk to him about that.

I help several more customers, watching the clock on the wall as I work. I just want Jamar to get here so I can go with Quentin to talk to the mechanic who worked on the Townsends' car. It's killing me that I don't have any answers, but at the same time, I feel justified that my suspicion that this wasn't merely an accident was correct.

Samantha comes up to the counter, making me wonder why she's back again. "I just saw your sister in Cam's place with the new guy in town."

Good. They did go to Cam's. "Yeah, they sort of hit it off."

"He's cute. I remember when I first saw him on Monday morning talking to Will, I thought, wow."

"You saw Wes talking to Will Townsend on Monday morning?"

"Yeah, and Will was an okay looking guy, but with him scowling at Wes, it just made Wes look even more good-looking."

"You think Will was unhappy with Wes?"

"Looked that way."

Wes just moved to town. What on earth could he have done that would upset Will? "Do you know what they were talking about?"

Samantha shakes her head. "No. I didn't hear what

they were saying. I just saw them through the window of my flower shop. Wes looked calm, but Will was irate. His jaw was clenched and everything.

There's only one way to find out what Wes said to upset Will. I need to interrogate my sister's new crush.

CHAPTER SEVEN

"Samantha, are they still at Cam's place?" I ask.

She bobs her head. "At least, they were a moment ago when I left."

I look at the clock on the wall again, and as if he could sense I needed him, Jamar walks into Cup of Jo.

"I know I'm a few minutes early, but I ate in the car on the way here. I couldn't wait to get started."

I want to dash next door before Mo and Wes leave, but I can't leave Jamar stranded here. I really need to show him how to use the coffee machines. "Come here. I'm going to show you how to make some drinks." I printed up instructions for each last night when I couldn't sleep, so I pull those out from under the counter where I put the pages this morning. I spend another hour with Jamar, which doesn't put me behind schedule to meet Quentin since Jamar got here earlier than we planned on. He's a quick learner. He only screws up one order, but I give the customer some free chocolates while he waits for Jamar to remake the drink correctly.

"I think I'm getting the hang of it," Jamar tells me.

"You're doing great," I say. "Just remember the steam wand has to stay submerged, or you'll have milk all over your apron."

"Speaking of apron's, I think I need a bigger size. Yours isn't exactly made for my height." He looks down at the apron that's struggling to fit around him.

"I'll order a larger one for you," I say. I look at the clock again.

"Do you have somewhere else to be?" Jamar asks. "You've looked at the clock no less than seven times since I got here."

I pull him toward the back room. "Can you keep a secret?"

"You know I can."

"Okay, I'm helping Quentin with the Townsend murder investigation."

Unlike with Samantha and Mo, Jamar doesn't blurt out the word "murder" for all my customers to hear. "I see. Well, then you should go. I can handle this. You left me instructions, and I've already practiced most of these drinks."

"If you get stuck, give the customer some free chocolates to keep them from complaining. We can afford to give away some chocolates."

"I'll be fine. I'll just do what I did yesterday." He does what I assume is a belly dance. "Unless you don't want me to do that."

"Just don't go dancing on any tables or removing any clothing, okay?"

He laughs, but when I don't, he says, "Oh, you're serious. I won't do anything like that. No worries."

"Great. My phone's always on, and I'll try not to be gone for too long."

"Don't look so guilty. You're paying me, remember?" He grabs my jacket from the hook under the counter and hands it to me. Then he turns me around and starts walking me to the door. "Hey, everybody, tell Jo we can survive for a little while without her," Jamar says in a loud voice.

"We're good, Jo!" someone yells.

I slip my arms through my coat sleeves. "Everybody, behave while I'm gone." I wag my finger in the air, but I smile at the same time.

Jamar shoos me out the door. As I head across the street to the mechanic's, I peek inside the windows of Cam's Kitchen. He has a few people inside, but Mo and the new guy aren't among them. I'll have to catch up to Wes another time. Mo is not going to be happy about it either.

I pull my phone out of my back pocket and call Quentin.

"Detective Perry," he answers.

"It's Jo. I'm walking to the mechanic's now."

"I'm already here. I'm parked on Second Street by where the accident took place. I didn't want Sam to see my car."

Because we both know she'd be over here right now trying to see what was going on if she knew Quentin was here. "I see you," I say, hanging up the phone. I walk over to him on the sidewalk. "Were you checking out the accident site again?"

"Yeah. Now it makes sense that there are no skid marks on the road. Will Townsend didn't use the brakes because he couldn't. They failed."

"Right after supposedly being fixed," I add.

"Are you thinking it was the mechanic who set this all up?" Quentin asks me.

"I'm not sure what motive he would have had to do so, but he had the opportunity for sure."

Quentin smirks. "Did you pick up the cop talk from me or from TV shows?"

It's from him. When we were dating, I became his sounding board, even though he wasn't supposed to be discussing cases with me. I'm pretty sure I've only ever served two purposes in Quentin's life: getting him closer to Samantha and helping him work through tough cases.

"Why don't we just go talk to the mechanic?" I say because I don't want to rehash the details of my time with Quentin.

He clears his throat. "Good idea."

We step in through the garage style doors, which are

both open. There are space heaters to keep the mechanics from getting cold, but the temperatures have been getting milder. I'm not even sure I need my coat today, but since I don't want to carry it, I leave it on.

Quentin walks up to the first mechanic he sees and flashes his badge. "Detective Perry with the Bennett Falls Police Department. I need to speak with the mechanic who worked on William Townsend's vehicle over the weekend."

"If it was Sunday, then you want Pete. He's the only one who works on Sundays." The guy points to a short, stocky man by the vending machine.

This is the only car shop I've ever known that's open seven days a week. I think it's smart because they have no other competition on Sundays.

Quentin leads the way over to Pete, who seems to be stuck mulling over his candy bar options.

"I'd go with the KitKat," I say.

Pete turns to look at me. "Thanks for the suggestion." He punches in B2, and the KitKat drops to the bottom of the machine, where Pete retrieves it. "I wanted a Snickers, but the machine is always out of them. It's a favorite around here." He opens the candy bar and takes a bite.

Quentin flashes his badge. "We understand you worked on William Townsend's car on Sunday."

"Yeah, I put new brake pads and rotors on it. Why?"

"Did you check the brake fluid?" I ask.

"I replaced the brake fluid. It really needs to be changed when you change the brakes."

Quentin looks ready to slaps some handcuffs on poor Pete. "And are you sure you replaced the brake fluid?"

"Of course. It wasn't my first time doing brakes. I've worked here for fourteen years."

"Screwups happen, though, right?" Quentin asks.

"Not to me, they don't. I tested the brakes myself. If I didn't replace the brake fluid, I would have crashed that car long before the Townsends got it back."

He makes a good point. "Are you sure you locked up the garage after you left on Sunday?" I ask.

"Simon's in charge of locking up for the night. He works in the office up front." He bobs his head toward the office. "He's here now if you want to talk to him."

"We do," Quentin says. "I might have some other questions for you as well, so don't leave town or anything."

Pete narrows his eyes. "Are you accusing me of something?"

"No," I say. "It's just that the Townsends' car had no brake fluid in it after the crash."

"Maybe it leaked out during the crash," Pete says. "I saw the front end of that car. It was demolished."

"Actually, it wasn't. The front end went into the old kitchen through a window. The driver and passenger were killed because part of the building's structure fell on top of the windshield and roof of the car, crushing them to death. The front end is banged up but not demolished." Quentin sounds like he's reading a school report, not talking about the way two people were killed. I don't know how he separates his emotions from these cases.

Pete crosses his arms. "Well, I know I put that brake fluid in there. You can ask Simon. He'll tell you my record is perfect. I've never had a single complaint or a job not done to the owner's satisfaction."

"Thanks, Pete," I say, pushing Quentin toward the office.

"What are you doing?"

"You have no evidence that he did anything wrong," I say. "Which means you can't hold him for questioning. If you want to get anything more out of him, you're going to have to play nice."

Quentin scoffs. "That's not really how investigations work, Jo. I don't close cases by playing nice."

"You didn't close the last case I helped you with. I did. So let's try it my way this time, okay?" I open the door to the lobby area.

"What are you doing? The office is over there," Quentin says.

"Yeah, and we're not barging in on the man. We're playing nice, remember? We'll ask for him." I walk up to the desk, and the receptionist looks up from the book she's reading.

"Can I help you?"

"Yes, we need to speak with Simon. We were told he's in today."

"Sure. Hang on." She picks up the phone on her desk and presses a button. "Simon, you have two people here to see you. Hold on. I'll ask." She lowers the phone slightly so it's under her chin. "Your names?"

"Jo Coffee and Detective Perry," I say.

Quentin whips out his badge. I swear it's his favorite toy. Give the man any reason to pull it out and show it off.

"Jo Coffee and Detective Perry," she says after bringing the receiver back to her mouth. "Okay." She hangs up. "You can go on in. It's that door there." She points to the room behind the receptionist's desk.

"Thank you," I say, knowing Quentin won't.

I knock on the door and wait for Simon to invite us in, which he does immediately. He doesn't get up from his desk when we enter the office. Instead, he keeps typing on his computer. "What can I do for you both?" He motions to the chairs opposite him.

I sit, but Quentin remains standing. I've seen him use this intimidation technique before, and even though I'm not sure it works, he sticks with it.

"One of your mechanics worked on the vehicle that was involved in the crash Monday morning. We discovered there was no brake fluid in the vehicle after the crash. We need to figure out how that happened."

"Your guess is as good as mine. It's standard procedure to test drive all vehicles before returning them to the customers. I know for a fact that Pete test drove the Townsends' car after he changed the brakes. There's no way he forgot to replace the brake fluid. The fluid must have leaked out at the time of the crash."

"We're certain that's not the case."

"Then I'm not sure what to tell you." Simon turns to face us for the first time and laces his hands in front of him. "Sorry I can't be of any help."

"You lock up before leaving every night, correct?" I ask.

"Naturally. It's a pretty safe town, but I'm not about to get sued for someone stealing a car from my shop."

"Does anyone else have a key to the shop?"

"No. Just me."

But locks can be picked. "Was there any sign that someone tampered with one of the locks?"

"No. Everything was locked up tight when I got here Monday morning."

"And the Townsends' car was exactly where Pete had left it?" I ask.

Simon nods. "I assure you nothing happened to that car while it was on the premises."

Then how did it lose all its brake fluid by the time Will drove it out of here? "You don't happen to have security cameras, do you?"

"No. We're locked up tight. Never had a break-in. I'm insured, though. I don't see the point in paying for security cameras on top of that."

"Well, you might now," Quentin says. "Because either your mechanic made a big mistake that caused the deaths of two people, or someone got in here and tampered with that vehicle. Either way, you've got a problem on your hands."

Simon stands up so he's about the same height as Quentin. "Are you charging me or Pete with something?"

"Not yet," Quentin says.

"Then I think we're done here," Simon says.

"Thank you for your time," I say, even though there's really no smoothing over the tension Quentin created in this small office. I get up and walk out.

"He has to be lying," Quentin says as we walk back outside. "Someone tampered with the brakes on that car."

"How do we prove it? And what motive would Pete or Simon have for doing that? Do either of them even know Will and Cynthia outside of working on their car?"

"Maybe Cynthia was having an affair with one of them and they wanted to get Will out of the way. It was his car. They might not have thought Cynthia would be in the car with him when he picked it up."

"That's a big risk to take with the life of someone you care about," I say. "And if she was having an affair with one of them, she would have mentioned her car dying. I mean, they work in a car shop. It would only make sense to bring it up on the off chance they could fix it for her."

"What does that leave us with then?" Quentin asks me, looking down the street to the gaping hole in the side of the building.

An idea hits me, and I hurry back inside.

"What are you doing?" Quentin asks, rushing after me.

"Is Simon still in his office?" I ask the receptionist. She picks up her phone to call him, but I keep walking straight to the office door and open it. "Did Will Townsend pay his bill?" I ask.

Simon looks more than a little annoyed that I let myself back into his office, but he reaches for a file on his desk and pulls out a check. "He wrote a personal check, which I tried to cash immediately after the accident."

"Afraid if you waited, the Townsends' account would be frozen once the bank learned of their deaths and you wouldn't get paid?" I ask.

Simon doesn't even try to deny it. "It didn't matter anyway because the account had nothing in it. I couldn't cash the check."

Then the question remains: was the account bled dry from paying the medical bills for Cynthia's mother, or did either Cynthia or Will empty it because they were leaving town?

"Did the teller give you any information as to why the account was empty?" I ask.

"They wouldn't tell me that. Just said sorry and I'm out of luck. A lot of good that does me."

I nod and walk back out.

Quentin grabs my arm. "Jo, what's going on in your head?"

I shrug my arm free. "I can't help thinking they were running away."

"What makes you think that?"

"Both were on edge that morning. They had their suitcases in the trunk. They could have emptied their account. Cynthia had money on her. She gave me that twenty-dollar bill to pay for her coffee." I tick each item off on a finger.

"She would have had to close the bank account on Saturday. I'll look into it to see if that's true."

"This is a small town. Someone has to know what was really going on with them. And someone has to know where they spent Sunday night."

"I can check with the bed and breakfast, too. See if they stayed there." Quentin jots some notes in his pad and shoves it back inside his jacket. "Thanks for your help, Jo. I'll let you know if I need you again."

While it bothers me that he just decides when my help is needed and when to toss me aside, I don't really want him with me while I question people. I don't want people to clam up and not talk because he's there. And I don't want to have to follow police procedure either. So, I just nod and start walking toward Cam's Kitchen.

"Jo," Quentin calls after me.

I turn around but keep walking backward since the crosswalk signal is on. "Yeah?"

"What are the odds you're going to listen to me and wait until I call you?"

I smirk and wave before jogging to make it across the road before the traffic light changes. I go inside Cam's

Kitchen. "Are you closing for the day?" I ask, watching Cam count out his register.

"Yup. Everyone's next door." Cam dips his head in the direction of my coffee shop.

Mickey was right. I'm the one who's driving Cam's bakery into the ground. And I just hired Jamar, who is bringing in even more traffic to Cup of Jo.

CHAPTER EIGHT

I move to the wall and place my hand on it. "Hear me out. I want to revisit the idea of knocking down this wall between our shops," I say. "Just the wall. Everything else will stay the same, but the two places will be connected. Maybe if we sell your baked goods with my coffee, we'll get more sales. I mean it's stupid not to work together when what we're selling goes together like…"

"Coffee and baked goods?" he asks with a sad smile.

"Yes." I move toward him. "Cam, this makes sense. You know it does."

"You want to partner our businesses?"

"Yeah, is that so awful?" I ask since he doesn't look the least bit enthused.

"We've only been dating for a few weeks. Don't you worry about what might happen down the road?"

"Why? Are you planning on cheating on me with my best friend?" I ask with a smirk. "Because Quentin beat you to that. But seriously, Cam, you and I have always been close friends. If this doesn't work out between us—and full disclosure, I really think it has a great shot at lasting—I'm not willing to lose you as my friend."

"I suppose it's a hurtle we can tackle if we come to it."

"Is that a yes?"

"It's a yes from me, but we have to convince the landlord. If he goes to resell the place or even lease it to someone else one day, he's down one store."

That's true. It might take some convincing. It's also going to cost money to remove that wall. "What if we don't remove the wall, but we put in a door? Like the ones in hotel suites so you can join two rooms?"

"And lock the door if you don't want to join them," Cam says, finishing my thought.

"Exactly. That has to be a lot less expensive. I can pay for it to be done."

"We'll split the cost. My business might not be off the ground yet, but if we're partnering up in anyway, I'm contributing an equal share of everything."

"Honestly, with it being a door we can open and close, we can keep two separate businesses, but it will encourage customers to buy from both places once they're here. If a customer wants a pastry with their coffee, I'll call you and you can deliver the pastry and vice versa. Or better yet, we can hire a waiter or waitress to go between the two shops."

"Okay, slow down. You're getting really excited about

this, and we don't even know what the landlord is going to say. He might shut down the idea immediately."

"Let's call him and find out."

"Now?"

I nod and dial Mr. DiAngelo. I blurt out the idea as quickly as possible so he can't cut me off. He isn't thrilled, but I knew it would take convincing.

"These two locations are small, Mr. DiAngelo. They're basically half the size of the others on the strip."

"That's because I divided one store into two," he says. "I paid for that construction to be done so I could lease another space."

"Are we paying the same amount as everyone else?" I ask.

"No. You pay based on the square footage. I'm not trying to rip anyone off."

"Then you don't actually make more money by splitting the location in two," I say.

"No, not exactly, but I thought more stores would bring more business to the strip as a whole, and I wasn't wrong. So in a way, I am making more money because I keep the leases for longer when the stores do well."

Except Cam's place isn't doing well. "What if I pay for the construction?" I say.

"Jo means she and I will split the cost," Cam says. "It wouldn't cost you anything. And with her idea of the door in between, you could separate the stores down the road."

Mr. DiAngelo doesn't say anything for a few minutes.

"Let me think this over. I'm not saying no. You know I like you two, and I don't want to lose Cam. I'll call you later this evening with my decision."

"Thank you, Mr. D.," I say.

"Yes, thank you," Cam says before I hang up.

"You know, we could get more tables in here to accommodate more eat-in customers. That might be the problem. Mickey parks his butt at one of my tables every day and—"

Cam stops my rant with a kiss. "Thank you for trying to help keep my business afloat. I don't know how to repay you for everything you're doing."

"How about helping me interrogate Mo's new love interest without her finding out?" I say.

"What?"

"Samantha saw Wes talking to Will Townsend on Monday morning, and from her perspective, it was a heated conversation."

Cam furrows his brow. "That doesn't make sense. I met Wes today when he came in with Mo. He said he just moved to town on Saturday. How would he even know Will?"

"No way!" I cover my mouth with my hand. "You don't think Wes is renting the house the Townsends used to live in, do you?"

"That would certainly cause tension between them," Cam says.

"Through no fault of Wes's," I say, although I'm not sure if I really believe he didn't do anything wrong or if I don't want to believe he did since I know my little sister likes him.

"You want to go visit Mo at her office?" he asks me. "You know you can't do this behind her back. You might as well go to the office and get it all out in the open."

He's right, and I hate keeping things from her. "Will you come with me?"

He nods. "I'm ready to close up anyway." He pushes in a chair and frowns.

I lace my fingers through his. "We might be getting good news later today."

"Yeah." He nods, but he doesn't look or sound convinced.

I check in quickly with Jamar, who is struggling with a cappuccino.

"Sorry, the foam and steamed milk mixed, and it just doesn't look right," he says.

"It's okay. You're just pouring it into the espresso too quickly." I steam some milk, waiting until it's hot enough and then pull up on the milk to create a nice froth on the top. "Okay, you want to hold the milk at more of an angle to keep the foam in the cup and only allow the milk to go into the espresso." I demonstrate it. "Now I'm left with just the foam to put on top." I finish making it and turn to hand it to Mrs. Marlow. "Here you go. On the house. Sorry for the wait."

Mrs. Marlow smiles at me and then pats Jamar's cheek. "I don't mind waiting. It means I get to stare at this face a little longer." She puts a five-dollar bill in the tip mug.

"Thanks for the help," Jamar says. "I promise I haven't been screwing up all day. It was just that one."

"Jamar, it's your second day. You're doing great. Really."

"I think I got rattled when a bunch of teachers came in. They were talking about the Townsends. It was tough listening to how much they missed Cynthia."

"Did any of them mention missing Will?"

Jamar shakes his head. "Cynthia was the outgoing one. Will was more reserved. He kept to himself. But I did hear one woman say her boss is still out because she's so upset by the news. She couldn't believe they both died. Said it was the worst tragedy the school had seen since she started working there."

"I think I know who you're talking about. She was out when I visited the school yesterday. I imagine there are a lot of upset individuals there."

"Yeah, they were all crying. I'm a sympathetic crier." He lowers his head.

"There's no shame in that. It's actually really sweet."

Cam claps a hand down on Jamar's shoulder. "Only real men cry."

I smile at him in gratitude. "Jamar, are you okay now? I have to run across the street to talk to Mo for a little bit."

"Yeah. I'm good. Thanks for showing me the trick with the cappuccinos."

"No problem. I should have been clearer in my instructions."

"You can dock my pay for Mrs. Marlow's drink."

"No need. She tipped five dollars. That covers the drink."

Jamar looks at me and then Cam. "You might be the best boss ever. Hang on to this one, Cam."

"That's the plan," Cam says.

With a wave to Jamar, we leave Cup of Jo and head to Mo's office. Just my luck, there's a tall blond man sitting on the edge of her desk, clearly flirting with her. I knock on her open door. "Hi."

"Jo, what are you doing here?" Mo asks, and when Wes turns to face me, Mo dips her head in his direction as if I haven't already figured out who he is.

"You're the famous Joanna Coffee," Wes says, standing up and offering me his hand. "Wesley Hart."

"Nice to meet you, Wesley." After shaking his hand, I say, "I believe you've already met my boyfriend, Cam Turner."

"Yeah, hey." Wes gives Cam a chin bob in recognition. "Really awesome crumb cake, man. I think I'm going to have to start coming to your place for lunch every day."

"Thanks, but—"

"You know, I heard a rumor," I say, cutting off Cam before he can tell Mo and Wes that Cam's Kitchen might not be open for much longer.

"What rumor?" Mo asks, looking afraid of what I

might say. And while I know she isn't going to like this, it's not because I'm about to embarrass her. No, I'm going to do something much worse.

"Yeah, I heard someone just rented out the two-bedroom cottage on Lake View Road. Was that you, Wes?"

"Um, yeah. Wow, news travels fast in this town."

I bob my head. "Small towns are like that. Did you meet the previous tenants of the house?"

Wes looks down at his shiny black shoes. "I did. Well, the husband at least. I didn't meet his wife. She was in your coffee shop, I think."

"Jo?" Mo's one-word question is loaded with accusation. She wants to know exactly where I'm going with this.

"Yes, she was. She was really distracted, too. Like something was wrong. She paid in such a hurry she didn't even allow me enough time to give her the change."

"Her husband was outside waiting for her. He was pretty agitated. He saw me and sort of went off about how I'm the reason they lost their house." Wes looks up at me. "I swear I had no idea they were kicked out. I just needed a place to live and quick. I got hired here, and I was told to start Monday, but I lived over two hours away. I couldn't commute."

"No, it's not your fault," Mo says, giving me a look that's nothing short of *Agree with me, and now!*

"Oh no, no one could possibly expect you to know

the previous tenants were evicted. How could you?" I say.

"I guess that guy saw me moving in. He told me who he was and blamed me for having to leave town."

"Did he actually say he was leaving town?" I ask.

"Yeah. Why?"

I look at Cam. There's one question answered. The Townsends were definitely leaving Bennett Falls. But why didn't they tell a soul other than Wes?

"Did he say where they were going?"

Wes shakes his head. "And I didn't ask. I just apologized even though I don't think I did anything wrong."

"You didn't," Mo says.

"No, you definitely didn't," I say because I'm convinced something else made the Townsends leave town. "But anyway, Mo, I was coming to say I can't do dinner tonight. I'm sorry to cancel on you on such short notice. I hope I'm not leaving you with nothing to eat." My acting skills are admittedly the worst, but I don't think Wes did anything to the Townsends, and Mo is clearly not happy with me stopping by and interrogating him, so I have to do something to make up for it. "Maybe you could show Wes around town. You know, point out the local hotspots and grab a bite to eat." I turn to Wes. "Unless you already have plans, in which case I'll feel awful for bailing on Mo." My acting skills are terrible, but the look on Wes's face says he's very open to the idea of spending more time with my sister.

"No. I have no plans," Wes says, turning to Mo. "I'd love it if you'd show me around, and I'd be happy to buy you dinner in return for the favor."

"That sounds great," Mo says.

"Oh good. I'm so relieved. Wes, it was really nice meeting you. Mo, I'll talk to you tomorrow." I wave, and as I'm turning to leave, Mo mouths, "Thank you."

"That was nice of you," Cam says as we head back downstairs.

"I owed her one, and besides, now we know the Townsends were leaving without even telling their boss."

"Let me guess. You're going back to the school tomorrow."

"I have to. There's no way someone at the school didn't know about this."

"You think someone lied to you?"

I nod. "And I'm going to find out who."

After I close up Cup of Jo for the day, Cam comes over for dinner. Jamar passes even though I extend the invitation. He says he's helping Lance with some final preparations for Friday's grand opening. Cam and I are just finishing dessert, a marble cheesecake he brought from Cam's Kitchen, when his phone rings.

He checks the screen and says, "It's Mr. DiAngelo."

"Answer it," I urge, moving my chair closer to his so I can hear what Mr. DiAngelo has to say.

Cam answers the phone on speaker. "Hello, Mr. DiAngelo."

"Evening, Cam. Is Jo with you?"

"She is," Cam says, grabbing my hand and squeezing it.

"Good. I've thought over your proposition, and I don't like the idea of creating a door between the two spaces. No one is going to want to have a door connecting two businesses down the road from now when you've both moved on."

"We understand," Cam says. "Thank you for at least considering our idea."

"Not so fast there, Cam. I'm not finished yet." Mr. DiAngelo clears his throat. "If both of your businesses can withstand closing for about two weeks, I can have my construction guys come in and remove that wall I had put up years ago. I think the best option is to make the space into one place the way it was. Now, I understand that means you can't keep two names on it, and you two will have to work that out among yourselves, but this is my best offer."

"We'll take it," I say. "Two weeks is nothing."

"The construction isn't complicated. It's demolition on one wall that was added, so it's not supporting the structure to begin with. Then it's painting and you two decorating from there. You might even finish in under two weeks."

"That sounds perfect," I say.

"I'll add the cost onto your rent if that works for you. I can send you the quote via email."

"Please do," I say, squeezing Cam's hand.

"Talk to you both in the morning." Mr. DiAngelo hangs up.

"Why don't you look happy?" I ask Cam.

"I don't know. For some reason, I keep thinking about the Townsends. What if it was money that caused their deaths?"

"What do you mean?"

"What if they left town because they had nothing left? Maybe they had to move in with Cynthia's mother. I could see how that would stress out Will. He might have even resented Cynthia for them being penniless."

"You think they had a bad relationship because of it?" I don't know why I didn't consider that. It's something someone would surely be able to confirm for me, though.

"It's possible, right?"

"It is, but that's not us. We're going to be fine. We'll manage to keep two separate accounts despite not having two names on the store."

"We're keeping Cup of Jo. People love it."

"You can't make all the sacrifices. You'll wind up hating me." As soon as I say it, I realize Cam could be right about the Townsends. "What if Will was trying to get into an accident? I mean it was Cynthia's mother who caused them to get into debt. Maybe he wanted to get rid of Cynthia."

"Why not just divorce her?" Cam asks.

"Because there was no money to do that," I say. "He

could have seen this as the only way out of the marriage and the debt."

"But Will died, too."

"I know. That part could have been an accident. Or…" What if Will Townsend had been pushed to his limit and wanted to end it all. "What if it was a murder-suicide?"

CHAPTER NINE

Thursday morning, after writing out the specials board, I write another one that announces the shop will be closed for renovations for up to two weeks. It's causing quite a stir, and several people who have become my regulars are already wondering where they'll get their morning coffee until I reopen.

"Trust me. You'll love the new place once we tear down that wall," I tell Mickey, handing him an extra-large dark roast and a chocolate stick. "I mean wouldn't you love a nice scone to enjoy with that coffee?"

He nods. "A scone does sound good. You sure you want to mix business and pleasure, though? You and Cam are sort of the talk of the town these days, when people aren't discussing murders and whatnot."

"Murders?" I ask.

"Yeah, Samantha said the Townsends were most likely murdered."

I should have known Samantha was behind the rumor. We can't even prove someone tampered with the car yet. I'm going to have to give Quentin the heads-up that his fiancée is saying more than she should about the case.

Mickey leans over the counter toward me. "Cynthia had a feeling someone was watching her. I didn't think much of it before because I thought the accident was... well, an accident. But now that I know it was murder, I think she might have been on to something."

"What makes you think she thought she was being watched? Did she tell you that?" I ask as I ring up his order.

He hands me a ten-dollar bill. "No. I found this note in the trash can in Gayle Sawyer's classroom. It was from Cynthia."

Who writes notes anymore when you can text someone? Unless Cynthia wanted there to be physical evidence of this. "Don't you think it's odd that Cynthia would write a note? I mean why not use her phone?" I ask him.

"The school has a strict no-phone policy for students and teachers. The teachers have them on them for security reasons, but they aren't allowed to use them otherwise unless they go outside the building."

"Do you remember what the note said?"

"She said someone in a black truck was following her."

"But she didn't know who it was?"

Mickey shrugs. "She didn't say in the note if she did."

"What was the name of the teacher Cynthia wrote the note to?" I grab my phone and open to the Notes app.

"Gayle Sawyer. She teaches art."

I put the name in my phone. "Thanks, Mickey. I'll follow up with Gayle and see what she knows."

"So you're investigating another case, huh? You're making a habit of this, Jo. What happened to selling coffee?"

"Coffee's my first love, Mickey. It always will be. But I have to admit, I like putting clues together, and with the shop closing for a while for renovations, I'll need something to keep me busy."

"I think it's the caffeine that helps you solve crimes," Mickey says. "You might want to convince the BFPD to start their mornings with a healthy dose of your coffee. They might be more successful that way." He winks at me before bringing his coffee to his usual table.

Cam walks into the shop, holding his phone in the air. "Mr. DiAngelo sent the quote. It's actually not as bad as I thought it would be."

"That's great." I pour a small decaf coffee for Mrs. Oliver and ring her up before checking out the quote on Cam's phone. "Any idea when they're going to start?"

"Tomorrow."

"Wow, that's soon."

"Yeah, and this isn't the guy Mr. DiAngelo usually uses. It's someone else he knows, and he thinks he can have us back up and running in about a week. He said it's not load-bearing and there's no wiring or plumbing in these walls because it was added later on. It's easy. Most of the time will be spent spackling and repainting, which this guy said he'd do for us as well."

"Is that included in the quoted price?" I ask.

Cam nods.

"That's fantastic."

"I thought so, too. I'm going to pack up some things to get them out of the way for the contractor this morning. It won't take long, so if you're going to the school later today, I'll be happy to tag along to help."

"I'd love the help. Thanks." I lean toward Cam. "I just found out from Mickey that Cynthia thought someone driving a black truck was following her."

Cam's head bobs. "That would explain her behavior Monday morning."

"It would. Do we know if anyone who works at the car shop drives a black truck?" I ask him. If they do, that might mean we found the person who drained the brake fluid in Will's car.

"I have time to head over there and check."

"Let me know what you find out."

"Will do." He kisses me on the cheek. "Can I get a coffee to go?"

"Of course. What would you like?"

He scans the flavored coffees. "I think I'll go with mocha today."

I grab a large to-go cup and pour the coffee. "Here you go. Pick me up at lunchtime to head to the school?"

"You got it." He smiles before sipping the coffee. "Mmm, that's good," he says before walking out.

"Good morning, Jo," Mrs. Marlow says as she steps up to the counter.

"Good morning, Mrs. Marlow. Will you be having a cappuccino today?"

"Yes, please." She sets her purse on the counter as she waits. "Mickey tells me you're playing detective again."

"Mickey talks too much," I say, giving her a smile as I steam the milk.

She laughs. "That he does. But most people in this town do, so he fits right in. You know, that ex of yours doesn't know how lucky he is having your help after what he did."

"That's all in the past, Mrs. Marlow. I'm over it. Besides, I'm not helping for his benefit. I'm doing this for Cynthia Townsend. She looked so scared Monday morning. I feel like I owe it to her to find out what really happened."

"You're a good girl, Joanna Coffee," Mrs. Marlow says as I place her cup on the counter. She removes a dollar from her wallet and places it in my tip mug. "Can I get one of those chocolate sticks? I just love them."

I pull one from the cup on the counter. "There you go."

She pays for her drink and sits down at the table with Mickey. I love how the people in this town will sit and talk to anyone. It's like we're one big, mostly happy family. At least those of us who have lived here all our lives.

I wipe down the counter, just for something to do since it's already clean. My phone buzzes in my back pocket, so I pull it out. Cam's name and image fills the screen, and I can't help smiling at his picture. "What did you find out?" I answer, knowing he's at the mechanic's shop on the corner of Main and Second Street.

"No one who works here drives a black truck, but get this." He pauses, and I hear his shoes against the asphalt. He must be crossing the road. "There was a black truck here on Monday."

"At the same time the Townsends' car was in for repairs." I'm not sure if that's good or bad news. If the truck was there, it could mean this person wasn't responsible, or it could be further proof that someone was following Cynthia. But then again, there are plenty of black trucks on the road, so there's no way to know for sure if it's the same one.

"Simon wouldn't give me any information about who owns the truck since I don't exactly have a badge, but he did say it was in for a wheel alignment."

Anyone can request a wheel alignment, so that would be a perfect excuse to get the vehicle in at the same time as the Townsends', but why? It's not like this person could hide in the back of the truck until the shop closed for the night and then drain the brake fluid from Will's car. Could they?

"What kind of truck was it?" I ask.

"A Chevy Silverado."

The door to Cup of Jo opens, and Cam walks in. He pockets his phone and heads toward me.

"Did it have one of those truck bed covers?" I ask immediately resuming our phone conversation once he's standing in front of me.

"I'm not sure. I didn't think to ask. Why?"

"I had a crazy idea." I wave my hand in the air, dismissing the thought.

"I do know that the truck was dropped off Saturday night right before closing. Pete, the mechanic we talked to, said he brought it inside before they locked up for the night."

"We need to find out who owns that truck."

"You're going to tell Quentin, aren't you?"

"I don't see that I have any other choice." I let out a deep breath and dial Quentin.

"Detective Perry," he answers on the third ring.

When is he going to put my number back in his phone? It's ridiculous that we dated for five years and he doesn't know it's me when I call. "It's Jo," I say, my tone showing my annoyance. "I have a lead for you." I step toward the back storage room even though there aren't any customers near the counter. "I need you to go to the mechanic's on the corner of Main and Second and find out who dropped off the black Chevy Silverado on Saturday night. Cam and I think the owner of that vehicle was following Cynthia Townsend."

"What makes you think that?" he asks.

I tell him what I learned from Mickey. "I'm going to talk to a few of Cynthia's friends to see if anyone knows anything more. I'll keep you posted."

"Jo, I have another case I'm working on at the moment that has to take precedence, but I'll follow up about the vehicle. Don't go getting yourself into any trouble, you hear me?"

"Cam will be with me. No worries." I hang up before he can give me a lecture.

I glance at the clock on the wall. I have about an hour before Jamar shows up for his shift. I'm sort of hoping that once the remodel is done, I can hire someone to serve as well. Or maybe Jamar will be willing to work here full-time. Not that I plan to make solving cases a habit, but it would be nice to not be tied to the shop all the time—to have a little freedom.

Mo comes in with a huge smile on her face. She marches up to me and gives me a hug. "Thank you, thank you, thank you."

"A take it your date with Wes went well," I say.

"So well. He's amazing, Jo. Like seriously amazing." She's practically bouncing on the balls of her feet.

"That's great."

"I need coffee." She scans the flavor options.

"I'm not sure you do. You're insanely hyper."

"I know. Isn't it fantastic? I swear I haven't had a sip of caffeine yet today. This is just me being happy."

"I'm happy for you, Mo."

She points to the amaretto coffee. "That one please."

I grab a small to-go cup, because she really does not need to fuel her giddiness, and pour the coffee. I hand it to her, and she adds cream and sugar before sipping it, nodding, and placing a cap on top.

"We have plans again tonight. Can you believe it? Two dates in two days."

"I'm assuming you invited him to Lance's grand opening tomorrow night, too," I say.

"Yes! Oh, you're right. Three dates in three days." She bobs up and down again.

"Easy girl. You just met him. Don't rush into things."

"I know. It's just that I haven't hit it off with someone like this in a long time. He's a really good listener. He asked all about you and Cam and...well, everything. He wants to know all about me."

"Where is he now?" I ask.

"Getting his car. We're going to lunch. I promised to show him the good lunch spots in town, too."

"Speaking of good lunch spots..." I fill her in on the remodel Cam and I will be starting tomorrow.

"That's great. I don't know why you two didn't do that from the start. Everyone knew you guys would end up together eventually. It just makes sense."

"I'm just glad Mr. DiAngelo was on board with the idea. It couldn't have worked out better."

Outside, a black truck pulls up in front of my door.

"Oh, that's Wes now," Mo says, waving as if Wes can see her through the front window.

My pulse quickens as I watch my little sister look happier than I've seen her in years while she waves to her new crush standing beside the vehicle I'm trying to track down. "Wes drives a black Silverado?"

"Yeah. Nice, right?"

No. Not nice. I thought I'd cleared Mo's new love interest of being involved in the murder. This discovery just put him back at the top of my suspect list.

CHAPTER TEN

I reach for Mo's arm. "You know, maybe I'll go with you guys to lunch," I say, not wanting to let Mo go anywhere with Wes if there's even a remote chance he's the killer.

She tugs her arm free and gives me a look. "What's up with you? You know this is a date."

I have to tell her the truth. She needs to be prepared. "Okay, Mo, I know you aren't going to want to hear this, but we believe someone who drives a black Chevy Silverado was following Cynthia Townsend and may have tampered with Will's car to cause the accident."

She laughs. "And you think that someone is Wes? Jo, come on. He just moved to town. He didn't even know Will and Cynthia."

"That's not exactly true. He and Will had an argument Monday morning."

"No, they didn't. Will yelled. Wes was a perfect gentleman." She places her hand on my shoulder and looks me in the eye. "Trust me. He's not the guy you're looking for. He's the guy *I'm* looking for."

"But, Mo, you don't know him. You don't know that he's a good guy."

"No, *you* don't know that, but *I* do. I get that you're just trying to look out for me because you love me, but I'm a big girl. I can handle myself." She lets go of me. "I'm going now. Thanks for the coffee."

She walks out, and since I can't exactly tackle her to the ground to stop her, I have no choice but to watch her get into Wes's truck and drive away.

Jamar walks in, and you'd think a local celebrity stepped into Cup of Jo. All of my customers go over to talk to him. He's smiling as he approaches me, but his face falls when he sees I'm upset. "What's wrong, Jo?"

"I'm worried about Mo. She's dating the new guy in town, and I'm not sure he's a good guy." I don't want to share any more details with Jamar just yet, so I leave it at the concerned big sister angle.

"I see. Want me to offer him a free training session? I could grill him for you, and that way Mo won't get mad at you for giving her new guy the third degree because I'd be doing it for you."

"That's sweet of you, Jamar, but I'm not sure how to introduce you to him and pull that off without Mo figuring out exactly what we're up to."

He nods as he ties on his apron. "You're right. She'd probably see right through it. Tell you what. If they come in here when you're not around, I'll play it off as trying to welcome the new guy to town. If you aren't around when I do it, Mo might not get suspicious."

"Smart thinking. Thanks, Jamar. You really are a great friend."

"And employee, I hope."

"Of course, and speaking of that, I'm going to close for renovations starting tomorrow. We're tearing down the wall between here and Cam's Kitchen to make it one place."

"Oh. How long will you be closed?"

"Probably about a week. It's an easy demo and painting kind of job. We'll be back up and running in no time. And yes, you're still going to work here. In fact, I'm going to need more help because Cam will be baking and we'll be having more eat-in guests to serve."

Jamar smiles. "Oh good, because I really love working here."

I place a hand on his shoulder. "You've got a job here for as long as you want it."

"Thanks, Jo."

I remove my apron and store it under the counter. "I have to go."

"More investigating?"

"Yeah, I'll fill you in tonight at dinner if you're coming. I'm just making tacos. Nothing fancy."

"I love tacos. I'm there, and I'll bring the margarita mix."

"Great! Maybe I'll invite Mo and Wes. Mo loves margaritas."

Cam walks into Cup of Jo, right on time.

"Gotta run," I tell Jamar before hurrying to Cam. The sun is strong today, and since the temperature is mild, I forgo wearing my jacket.

"Did I see a black truck out here earlier?" Cam asks. "It was pulling away when I came out of the kitchen."

"Yeah, you did," I say, climbing into Cam's SUV. I wait for him to get in before saying more. Once the car is in drive and he's pulling onto the road, I say, "Wes owns a black Chevy Silverado, and he was picking up Mo for lunch."

"You're not kidding, are you?" he asks, giving me a worried look.

"I wish I were. He's new to town, so Cynthia wouldn't have known who he was if he was following her. He drives a black Chevy Silverado. It all lines up, Cam."

"But how would he know Cynthia? What would make him target her?"

"I don't know. We need to run Wes's name by Gayle Sawyer to see if he could be Cynthia's stalker."

"You think she was being stalked?"

"What else could it be?" I ask.

"Well, they had money issues, so I was thinking maybe someone they owed money was following them to see if they were doing anything like going out for lavish meals or something that would point to them lying about being broke."

"Let me see if Quentin was able to follow up with the bank yet." I pull out my phone and dial Quentin.

"Bad time, Jo. I'm about to interrogate a kid who is supposedly selling drugs in his neighborhood."

"I'm surprised you knew it was me," I say.

"I figured it made sense to put you back in my phone."

"I just have a quick question for you. Were you able to confirm that the Townsends were in fact broke?"

"Yeah, I spoke with the bank this morning. The account was empty. All the money had been spent on her mother's medical bills judging by the checks Cynthia wrote out."

"According to Rudy Wilcox, Cynthia's mother is out of the hospital now. Maybe she knows something."

"You talked to the Townsends' landlord?" Quentin huffs into the phone. "What am I saying? Of course, you did. Anyway, I'll follow up with her mother. You worry about that coffee shop of yours."

I don't bother to tell him my time is freeing up thanks to the renovation. "Good luck with your interrogation," I say and end the call.

Cam is parked in the school lot by the time I finish talking to Quentin. "Any clue where we're going?" he asks me as we get out of the car.

"Main office. We'll ask for Gayle and go from there."

Once again, I go through the process of being buzzed in, having my driver's license scanned, and signing in. The security guard tells us to have a seat while he calls Gayle's classroom.

I recognize Katrina Davis, the secretary I spoke

with last time I was here, come out of the office into the hallway where Cam and I are seated in chairs lining the one wall. She looks frazzled. "Hello, Ms. Davis," I say.

She narrows her eyes at me as she says hello, and I know she's trying to place my face.

"I'm Joanna Coffee. We spoke the other day about Cynthia and William Townsend."

"Oh, yes. They're all I ever talk about this week. It's been absolutely crazy with the grief counsellors, getting coverage for all the classes, and dealing with staff members calling out."

"It's only been a few days. I'm sure things will get better next week."

"I hope so. I don't mean to be callous when people are clearly grieving, but I can't keep doing the work of multiple people each day." She looks down at the file folder in her hands. "Oh, who are you here to see? It's not me, is it? Because I have to get this file to the guidance department and then go cancel two meetings for the principal."

"No, we're here to see Gayle Sawyer."

She couldn't look more relieved. "Good." She takes a few steps down the hall, pauses, and turns back to me. "It's funny because of all Cynthia's friends, she was closest to Gayle. That's who I'd think would take the week off, not some of the other staff members."

"Maybe she's the type who needs to stay busy when she's upset," Cam suggests. "Idle time allows the mind to focus on things some people want to forget or move on from."

"You could be right," she says. "Anyway, I've got to run."

"She seems nice enough," Cam says. "Stressed but nice."

I nod.

A woman in her mid-thirties wearing a black pencil skirt and a deep purple top comes walking toward us. Her dark hair is in a bun, held by two paintbrushes. Call me presumptuous, but I'm going to guess she's Gayle Sawyer, the art teacher. I nudge Cam's arm with my elbow before standing up. "Ms. Sawyer?" I ask.

"Yes, and you are?"

"I'm Joanna Coffee, and this is Camden Turner. We knew Cynthia and Will Townsend." Knew them, knew *of* them—it's not that big of a difference, right?

"I see. Since you're here, I'm assuming you know I was close to Cynthia."

I nod. "Is there somewhere we could go to talk in private?"

"I was just eating lunch in my classroom. You're welcome to join me."

"Thank you."

Since we already have our visitor's badges, we follow her down a hallway to our right.

"I always had lunch in my classroom with Cynthia. Sometimes Erica Daniels would join us. She works in the art department too, but she teaches sculpture.

Cynthia and I don't care for the teachers' lounge very much. It's crowded and loud. Plus, Cynthia liked the smell of the paints." She gives a sad laugh, and a tear escapes her left eye and trails down her cheek. She quickly wipes it away. "I'm sorry. It's been a tough few days."

"I can imagine. I saw Cynthia Monday morning right before the accident." I decide it's best to keep calling it that for the time being.

"You did?" Gayle pauses before opening a classroom door.

"Yes, she seemed nervous."

"That was Cynthia's usual state lately. Between her mother's hospitalization and then…" Her voice trails off.

"And then what?" I ask.

She looks down the hallway, and even though it's deserted, she says, "You better come inside."

I step into the room, which does smell like paint. Only I don't like the smell the way Cynthia did. I'm not sure I'd want to eat my lunch in here, and certainly not every day.

"I know what you're thinking," Gayle says. "Cynthia was crazy for liking this smell, but she actually had a terrible sense of smell. She got a head injury as a child, and her sense of smell never fully recovered from it."

"What kind of head injury?" Cam asks, looking around at the paintings on the easels.

"She was knocked off a horse. She landed on her head, so really, she was lucky to be alive. The paint fumes are strong enough that she could smell them. I think it made her feel more normal."

She sits down at a table in the back of the room where her lunch container is sitting, the contents half-eaten. "I'm afraid I don't have anything to offer you."

"That's okay. We're fine," I say. "We're actually hoping you can give us some information."

"What kind of information?" She takes another bite of her chicken salad.

"I know Cynthia thought someone who drove a black truck was following her. Did she have any idea who that might have been?"

"I didn't know Cynthia had told anyone else about that." She puts down her fork, and I wait for her to continue. "I never saw a black truck in the parking lot here, and the time she asked me to drive her home, I didn't see it on her street either, but she said it was there most of the time. She saw it."

"And she didn't think it belonged to anyone who lived on the same street?" Cam asks.

Gayle shakes her head. "She said it was always idling somewhere different on the road. It was never parked in anyone's driveway." Tears fill Gayle's eyes again. "I should have believed her, but I never saw the truck or anyone following her. I thought she was just under a lot of stress because of her mom and then losing the house. I even talked to her landlord. Begged him to let them stay a little longer."

"So, you didn't think she was being followed?" I ask.

"It doesn't matter if she was or not. I was her best friend, and I dismissed her concern. Even if she was losing it because of everything that was going on, I should have been there for her. I should have said I believed her even if I didn't. And after that voice mail…"

"What voice mail?" I ask.

"She called me Monday morning. She said she was with Will, and she felt like someone was following her."

"Did she notice anyone who looked suspicious?" Cam asks.

"She was hysterical in her message. I could barely make out the words."

"Do you still have the voice mail?" If she didn't delete it, it might give us a clue.

Gayle stands up and walks to the desk in the front of the room. "I'm not supposed to use my phone inside the building."

"Yes, I heard about that rule," I say. "If I give you my number, would you forward the message to me?"

"Sure." She grabs a sketch pad and a charcoal pencil and hands them to me.

I jot down my number and give them back. "Is there anything else you could tell us about this truck or who might own it?"

She shakes her head. "Cynthia thought it could have been someone from her past."

"Why did she think that?" Cam asks.

"Well, she said she had something similar happen to her in high school. This boy in the grade below hers liked to follow her around. He would even drive by her house late at night. She'd see his car. She knew it was him because he had lights that lined his license plate. Blue lights, she said."

"Do you know that boy's name?" I ask.

"Cynthia didn't even know his name. Only that people called him *Tool*. He wore a tool belt to school. It didn't have any tools in it because they weren't allowed, but he wore it anyway."

That's odd. Why wear an empty tool belt? "Gayle, do you know if the school keeps copies of old yearbooks?" I ask.

"Yeah, the library has them. I can walk you over there if you'd like."

"That would be great. Thank you."

She gets up and leads the way upstairs to the second floor. The library is smack in the center of the building, and it's huge.

Gayle approaches the man at the desk, whom I assume is the librarian. "A.J., this is Joanna and Cam. They'd like to see back issues of the yearbook," Gayle says. Then she turns to Cam and me. "I have to get back to my room before my next class. You can see yourself out since you're wearing visitor badges."

"Thank you for your help. And please send me that voicemail message when school gets out."

"I will." She turns and walks out of the library.

A.J. smiles at us. "Old copies of the yearbook are located in the back corner. Follow me." He brings us to a shelf that's full of yearbooks from the past few decades. "They're shelved by year, so just search for the years you're looking for." He gives us a nod and walks away.

"What year are we looking for?" Cam asks.

"Well, Cynthia was thirty-five, so she would have been eighteen in…" I pause to do the math in my head. "2003. But we don't know if she was a senior when that happened, so we might have to check as far back as 2001. That's as far as we can go since she'd be a sophomore and Gayle said this guy was a year younger than Cynthia."

"Let's start with 2003 and work our way back then." Cam scans the numbers with me.

They're arranged from newest to oldest, the oldest being on the lower shelves. I find 2003's yearbook and pull it from the shelf. We bring the book to the nearest table and sit down. Since I know his picture won't be labeled "Tool" I look through the clubs instead, looking to see if there's a technical education club of some nature. They didn't have one when I went to Bennett Falls High School, but that doesn't mean they didn't have it when Cynthia was here years before me. No luck. I start looking through the candid shots next, hoping to spot someone wearing a tool belt.

"There," Cam says, pointing to a small black-and-white photograph of a bunch of kids posing in front of a mural made up of music notes on the wall.

"Is that Cynthia?" I ask, pointing to the blond girl in the middle of the photo.

"And look at the corner of the shot," Cam says.

I squint at the grainy image of a scrawny boy wearing a tool belt. He's not looking at the camera. His gaze is trained on the group of girls. Though I'd wager it was on Cynthia alone. His face is in profile since his head is turned, which doesn't give us much to go off of.

Cam keeps his finger to mark the place in the yearbook where we found the photo, and then we flip to the junior class photos to try to find a match. Thirty minutes later, we still haven't matched the kid from the candid photo to anyone in the junior class.

"Look," I say, pointing to a list of names under the heading, "No photo." "He must be one of these."

Cam discreetly pulls out his phone and snaps two pictures. One of the list of names and the other of the candid photo with Tool in it.

"You're breaking school rules, Mr. Turner," I tease.

"I don't work here or attend this school anymore." He smiles at me and returns the yearbook to the shelf. "Come on. We can look these people up online and see who resembles the kid in the photo."

"Sounds great, but there's one problem."

"What's that?"

"What are the odds this guy looks anything like the scrawny teenaged boy in that photo?" I'm thinking not very good.

CHAPTER ELEVEN

It took about twenty minutes of begging to get Mo to agree to come over for dinner and not go out with Wes. Not that I think Wes is the guy we're looking for. He's too young. But Mo is our internet guru, and if one of us is going to find Tool, it's going to be her. The promise of margaritas helped win her over. I also mentioned that being available all the time would make Wes think she had no social life. So now she's seated at my kitchen table with her laptop.

"Why do some good-looking boys turn into men who don't care at all about personal hygiene or their health? What ever happened to aging gracefully? I mean, these guys are only in their mid-thirties. That's way too young to let themselves go like that." Mo turns her laptop screen to me as I set a bowl of shredded cheese on the table next to the other toppings for our tacos. "Take this guy for example."

The man in the photo looks like he hasn't showered or shaved in weeks. His shirt is stained and almost threadbare, and I'm pretty sure there's food stuck in his beard. "Eek. No way was he good-looking in high school," I say.

"Want to bet?" She pulls up another picture and places them side by side. In the second picture, the guy is in great shape, clean shaven, with perfect hair, and wearing a clean football uniform. He's holding his helmet, so I can see his chiseled jaw and adorable smile.

"That's the same guy?" I ask.

"Yup. Sad, right? I mean you marry this guy, and then one day you wake up next to that." She points to the second photo.

"Maybe he has a medical condition that caused him to put on weight and it makes it difficult for him to exercise or even shower," I suggest.

She pulls up another picture from the guy's Facebook photos. "Nope. In every other photo, he has a beer and/or potato chip bag in hand. This guy just doesn't care."

"What you're saying is this is going to be a lot harder than we thought," Cam says, pulling the tray of hard taco shells out of the oven.

"Much harder."

"Sorry I'm late," Jamar says, walking in with the margarita mix in hand.

"No problem. The blender is on the counter. Get to

work on those drinks. Cam and I are putting the food on the table right now."

Mo picks up her laptop and carries it to the coffee table. "Did you really think Wes was the killer?" she asks me as she sits down at the table.

"He drives the same vehicle," I say, taking my seat.

"We don't think it's him anymore?" Jamar yells over the sound of the blender crushing the ice.

I shake my head rather than yell back.

"Good, because I'm going to quit working at the gym," he says as if that has anything to do with Wes.

"You are? Why?" I ask.

He turns off the blender. "Well, you said you were going to need to hire someone to serve food and drinks when you combine Cup of Jo and Cam's Kitchen. I want to do it. I'm not the best at making the drinks, but I can be a server for sure."

"You might not be the best at making drinks, but you are by far the best entertainment," Mo tells him. "I could see part of the show you put on today from my office. You know when you were in the front of the coffee shop by the windows."

Jamar's face reddens. "I sort of took dance lessons as a kid. I know every kind of dance there is."

"As long as it's not pole dancing, you're welcome to keep entertaining my customers," I say.

He pours the margaritas and brings them to the table. "Don't worry. It's nothing inappropriate. Today, I was salsa dancing with Mrs. Ramos. She might be seventy, but the woman has some moves."

"When are you leaving the gym?" I ask. "I won't be open for at least a week."

"Next Friday, so I'll be ready to start when you reopen."

I look at Cam and smile. "Then I think I just need to hire one more person to help out with drink orders when I need to slip out."

"He or she might need to warm up some pies for me if I slip out with you," Cam says. "All the real baking will be done in the mornings before the shop opens."

"What will you call the place?" Mo says. "I'll be sad if it's not Cup of Jo anymore."

"We're keeping Cup of Jo," Cam says. "It will still be my kitchen, but I don't need it named after me."

"We can put the sign from your storefront above the kitchen itself or on the door," I suggest.

Cam starts prepping a taco. "That works for me. Now, let's eat because I'm starving."

After dinner, Jamar goes back to his place, and Mo, Cam, and I are on the couch, looking through current pictures of the students who weren't part of the junior class photos in the yearbook. We can't find a match. The grainy shot we got of Tool doesn't reveal eye color, hair color, or height since the shot was taken from the waist up.

I'm about to give up when my phone chimes with a text message alert. I look at the screen and don't recognize the number the message came from. I click on it to open the message. "Oh, it's from Gayle. This is the voice mail I asked her to send me." I click on it and immediately switch to the speakerphone.

Cynthia's voice comes through. "Gayle, he's here. It's just like high school. I can feel his eyes on me everywhere I go. Just a few minutes ago, I saw someone watching me from across the street. He had his hood up so I couldn't see his face, but when he noticed me staring at him, he started toward me. I ran into Cup of Jo. I don't know where he is now, but I know he's following me. I know it, Gayle. He came back for me."

"Let's go——" a male voice cuts in before the message ends.

"Was that Will's voice at the end?" Cam asks.

"Most likely. He sounded like he was in a hurry." I replay the message to make sure I didn't miss anything before I reply to Gayle to thank her. I also ask her if Cynthia thought she had a stalker like she did in high school or if she suspected it was the *same* stalker from high school. I don't want to waste our time looking for this Tool guy if he's a dead end. I've had enough of those on this case.

Her response is just to say she's not sure.

"I think it's time to call Cynthia's mother. Maybe Cynthia confided in her," I say. I don't want to get my hopes up, though, since her mother's been ill. Cynthia probably didn't want to make her mother worry on top of whatever health issues she was already dealing with.

"I'll look for her number. What's the last name?" Mo asks.

I look at Cam. "I don't know." Quentin does, I'm sure, but I don't want to ask him because he'll know what I'm up to, and he already told me he'd follow up with Cynthia's mother. I get an idea. I look up the number for Rudy Wilcox, the Townsends' old landlord instead.

"Hello?" he answers. "If you're a telemarketer, I'll be honest. I'm going to hang up on you."

"No, I'm not a telemarketer, Mr. Wilcox. This is Joanna Coffee. I spoke to you the other day about the Townsends."

"Oh, yes. I remember."

I'm tempted to ask how his new tenant is doing since I still don't know much about Wes and he's dating my sister, but since Mo is sitting right next to me, I focus on the real reason for my call. "I was curious if you knew Cynthia Townsend's maiden name." I should have thought to look her up in the yearbook as well.

"Um, hang on. I think she signed her full name on the lease. I remember because I think it's stupid when people hyphenate their names like that. Either change your name or don't." He ruffles through paperwork on the other end. "Here it is. Cynthia Jane Townsend. Oh, it's not hyphenated. My mistake. It must be her middle name."

"Thank you anyway, Mr. Wilcox." I end the call. "Mo, did you try her Facebook profile. Sometimes people list their maiden names, too, so old classmates can find them."

"Hang on." She types Cynthia Townsend into the search bar. "Man, that's a common name. You're going to have to give me a little time to look through these."

I refill my margarita glass, and Cam follows me to the kitchen. "You okay?" he asks me.

"Yeah. I don't know why I'm so wrapped up in this. I mean I'm not a cop. I run a coffee shop, but as crazy as it sounds, I feel like the fact that my to-go cups were in that car when it crashed was a sign I'm supposed to solve this case."

He takes my hands in his. "First, I'd never call you crazy. Second, this is our town. I get why you don't want to see anything bad happen to the people here. And since something did happen, you want to fix it in some way. In this case, the only way to fix things is to find out what really caused Will to crash the car."

"You always did get me, Camden Turner." I reach up on my toes and give him a kiss.

"Hey, love birds. I found her," Mo says.

We walk back to the couch where I see she has my phone.

"I looked up the number that texted you and found Gayle Sawyer. Then I went to Gayle's Facebook profile and found Cynthia Langley Townsend." She turns the laptop to face us.

"Great. Now we need to find out what her mother's first name is."

"I already did." Mo clicks on a picture of one of Cynthia's Facebook friends. "Gretchen Langley. She currently lives in a fifty-five-and-up community in Fort Myers, Florida."

"I don't suppose you got a phone number, too," I say.

"Her number's listed, yes."

"Perfect." I grab my phone and punch in the number on Mo's laptop screen. "You're the best. Thanks, Mo."

"I know, and you're welcome. Now if you don't need me, I think I'll go join Wes for a drink at the pub."

"I thought you were making yourself less available," I say.

She shrugs. "I'm only available for part of the night." She grabs her jacket off the kitchen chair and walks out.

"Hello?" comes a frail voice on the other end of my phone.

"Hello. Is this Gretchen Langley?"

"Yes. Who is this?"

"Mrs. Langley, my name is Joanna Coffee. I knew your daughter, Cynthia."

"Where is she? She hasn't called me in days."

Oh, God. How can she not know her daughter is dead?

"Hello?" she asks. "Are you still there?"

"Yes, Mrs. Langley. Didn't your other daughter call you?"

"She's flying out tomorrow. She said she needed to talk to me."

My guess is she wants to be with her mother when

she gets the news about Cynthia. It could mean Gretchen isn't well enough to handle her daughter's death on her own. I can't be the one to tell her. "Well, I'm sure your daughter will explain everything. I was calling because I'm trying to figure out if Cynthia was contacted by anyone from high school recently."

"Is there a reunion?"

Cynthia graduated in 2003, so her reunion wouldn't be until 2023, but I get an idea. "Yes, I'm with the planning committee. We like to start preparations a few years out. One of the men on the committee has been contacting people already. I wasn't sure if he'd spoken with Cynthia. He mentioned he'd be visiting Bennett Falls, and I know Cynthia still lives there."

"Oh, I don't know. I'm afraid I've been in the hospital. I had a heart attack. Needed surgery and everything. Cynthia is supposed to be driving down here. She said she'd be here by Wednesday." She pauses. "What day is it?"

I think quickly to come up with an excuse to get off the phone without having to answer that question and arouse suspicion. "Mrs. Langley, I'm very sorry, but I'm getting another call and I need to take it. Have a good evening." I end the call and look at Cam. "Cynthia and Will were driving to Florida the day of the crash."

"If they were going to see her mother, why wouldn't she tell anyone she worked with?" Cam leans back on the couch. "Why all the secrecy?"

I can think of a few reasons. "Maybe she was afraid

if she told people, her stalker would find out and follow her. He could easily locate her mother's place just like Mo did."

"That's true."

"Or maybe I'm right about Will. Maybe he didn't want to tell anyone because he had no intention of leaving town. Maybe it was just to get Cynthia in the car so he could crash and kill her."

"You still think the murder-suicide is an option?" Cam turns his head toward me.

"I don't know what to think. Gayle didn't believe Cynthia was really being followed. If her best friend didn't believe her, maybe it's because Cynthia was so distraught over her mother's heart attack and losing all her money that she was going crazy from it."

"Did Will grow up here, too?" Cam asks.

"I don't know, but I'm starting to think we should have spent more time looking at that yearbook."

"Are we heading back to the school tomorrow?" he asks.

"No. It will get back to Quentin if we keep showing up there. We can google William Townsend."

"What you're telling me is it's a romantic evening of online research," Cam says.

"You never knew dating me would be this exciting, did you?" I tease.

"Rise and shine, non-workers," Mo yells.

I open my eyes to see I'm still on the couch. The laptop is beside me, and I'm propped up against Cam. "We fell asleep researching?"

"Is this how all your dates end?" Mo asks me, pulling me to my feet. "And FYI, your boyfriend is not easy to wake up." She nudges his foot with hers. "Cam!"

"What?" His head jerks up, and he looks around. "What happened?"

Mo pushes me toward the bathroom. "You guys had a wild night, apparently. You left the door wide open and everything."

I brush my teeth and pat down my hair before going back out into the living room.

"I sent Cam home, so go shower. I'll throw some toast in the toaster."

"You don't put toast in a toaster. You put bread in the toaster, and it makes toast."

She waves a hand in the air. "I'll make coffee, too."

I take a quick shower and get dressed in jeans and a gray lightweight sweater. I smell the toast burning before I see it.

"Sorry," Mo says. "It was too light the first time, so I put it back in."

Jamar comes into the apartment. "Where's the fire?" he asks, fanning his face.

"No fire. Just Mo burning my breakfast," I say.

"Hey, it's not my fault you and Cam slept on the

couch and didn't wake up early enough to make me breakfast."

"Why is it my job to make you breakfast?"

"Duh. You shut down Cup of Jo. What else am I supposed to do?" She says it like I should have figured that out for myself.

"Speaking of sleeping on couches, Midnight is parked on mine, and I have to go to work. Can you see if she's gone when you leave, Jo, and, if so, shut my door for me?" Jamar asks.

"Of course."

"I'd love to know where she goes each night. That's the first time she's slept at my place."

"She's got her pick of apartments here," Mo says.

Their conversation makes me think of something I haven't considered for days. "Where did the Townsends sleep Sunday night?"

"Huh?" Mo asks.

I go to the coffee table to retrieve my phone, and I shoot a text to Gayle, hoping she isn't already at the school with her phone off.

"What are you doing?" Mo asks.

"See you, ladies," Jamar waves and rushes off to get to work.

"Cynthia and Will were already out of their house Sunday night. I meant to follow up with where they stayed that night because they didn't even have their car to sleep in."

"You think they stayed with Gayle?"

"No, I don't. I'm not sure who they stayed with. They didn't have money for a room at the bed and breakfast, though. I know that."

"Who else were they close to?" Mo asks.

"Erica Daniels, another teacher at the school. Then there's the woman in charge of attendance. She was close to both of them, I think. That's why she hasn't returned to work yet. She's grieving."

"Sounds like she knew them well, then," Mo says. "I'd go talk to her if I were you."

"You're right. That's exactly what I should do."

"Need me to look her up?" Mo checks her watch. "I have about twenty minutes to spare."

"Do you mind? Her name is Susan Bell." I search my memory to make sure that's correct. "Yeah, that's the name that was on her desk."

"Okay." Mo pulls her laptop from her bag and sits down at the kitchen table. "Susan Bell. Susan Bell. Got it. She lives on Lake View Road. That's weird."

"The same road the Townsends lived on. Why is that weird?" I ask, pouring myself a cup of coffee.

"I don't know. I guess it's more of a coincidence than weird." She shrugs. "It's house number one hundred twenty-seven. That's literally right next door to Wes's place."

"Thanks."

"You'll wait for Cam, right?" Mo asks.

I cock my head at her, not sure why she thinks I won't be safe on my own. "I'm just going to talk to one of the

Townsends' coworkers, but, yes, *Mom*, the plan is to go with Cam." I stress "Mom" to let her know I think she's being ridiculous.

"Hey, if you can be overprotective about who I date, I can be overprotective about you investigating police cases." She wags a finger at me, returns her laptop to its bag, and walks out.

Little sisters!

After taking care of Midnight and locking Jamar's apartment, I call Cam on my way to Lake View Road, but the call goes to voice mail. He must be in the shower. "Hey, Cam. I'm on my way to talk to Susan Bell. She works in the attendance office at the school and has been out all week. I'm guessing she was close to Cynthia and Will if she can't bring herself to go back to work yet. And she lives on the same road they did, too. Meet me at one-twenty-seven Lake View Road when you get this."

I disconnect the call with the Bluetooth as I turn onto Lake View. I don't get far before I see a black Chevy Silverado, and it's not Wes's because his is still parked in his driveway. The truck is across the street from Wes's house. I try to casually drive by and look out my window to get a better view of the driver, but the man has a pair of binoculars in front of his face. He catches me looking at him and drives away.

As stupid as I know it is to go after him alone when he might be the killer, I make a K-turn in the street and follow him.

CHAPTER TWELVE

I get close enough to the truck that I can see him look at me in the rearview mirror. I can't make out his features, though, so I still have no idea who he is. He turns down a side street and steps on the gas, despite all the turns on the road. Keeping pace with him isn't easy. As soon as we hit a straight stretch of road, he guns it. As much as I want to do the same so I don't lose him, I know there's a one-lane bridge coming up ahead. I'm not willing to take the chance that no one will be coming when I get there, so I only increase my speed a little bit. The gap between us widens, and he takes the next turn hard, kicking up all the dirt and gravel on the road.

I struggle to keep his truck in sight. I'm just getting around the turn when he speeds across the one-lane bridge, narrowly missing a car coming from the other direction. I have no choice but to slow to a stop and let the car cross. But it's not just one car. It's several, all with their headlights on even though it's broad daylight. It's a funeral procession. I can't cut into their line.

I lean my head forward on the steering wheel, knowing I've lost the truck.

My phone rings, and I press the button on the steering wheel to answer it. "Hello?"

"Where are you?" Cam says.

I finally lift my head. "I found the black truck and followed it to Sandalwood Road, but before I could follow him across the bridge, I got held up by a funeral procession."

"Why would you go after the truck on your own?"

"I couldn't just let him get away."

"You should have taken a picture of his license plate."

"Why? The car shop knows who he is, right? I can get Quentin to find out his name. I caught him with binoculars spying on Wes's house."

"Why would he spy on Wes's house?"

"I don't know." What I do know is it's time to tell Quentin everything. "I'll meet you at Susan Bell's house. I'll call Quentin on the way."

To say Quentin isn't pleased with me is an understatement, but he said he'd find out who owned the truck and then go question him. Without me. How's that for gratitude? And he wonders why I don't always share information with him on these cases.

Cam is parked out front of Susan's house when I arrive, so I pull over right behind his SUV.

"Quentin is going to get the name of the owner of that truck right now," I tell Cam.

"Good. Maybe this will all be over soon."

"In the meantime, let's see how well Susan knew Cynthia and Will. I'm guessing pretty darn well since they were neighbors and coworkers."

"It would seem that way."

I knock on the front door and wait. Susan answers wearing a silk robe. "If you're selling something, I'm not interested," she says, already closing the door on us.

"We're friends of the Townsends," I say.

She opens the door again. "Oh. What are you doing here?"

"We were at the high school talking to some of their coworkers, and we heard you were very close to Cynthia and Will. I imagine the news of their passing is very difficult for you."

"Yes." She sniffles and reaches into her pocket for a tissue. "I can't believe they're both dead. I mean, how?"

"I know it was awful, but we were hoping you could answer a few questions for us."

She dabs her eyes. "Questions? Why me?"

"Well, we know Cynthia and Will were kicked out of their house, and we're trying to find out where they stayed Sunday night."

"You found it. They were here."

Finally, some good luck in this case. "Did you know they were planning to go away?"

"Cynthia was going to see her mother, yes."

"But not Will?" I ask.

She shakes her head. "He was driving her to the airport."

"I see." How did they afford a plane ticket if they were broke? I'd think they'd drive. "I'm sorry, but something doesn't seem right. I know they were having financial troubles. I just would have thought they'd take the car to Florida."

"I paid for Cynthia's plane ticket. They didn't want to impose on me by asking me to purchase one for Will as well, so he was going to stay behind and look for a cheap place to rent. He was working two jobs, you know, to try to get them back on their feet."

Mickey was right about that. Will left work as soon as the school day ended so he could get to his second job.

"I've heard from a few other people that Cynthia didn't seem like herself lately because of everything going on with her mother. Did you notice the same thing?" I ask.

"It's only natural that she was worried about her mother. It left Will to worry about the finances."

"Yes, I suppose that does make sense," I say. "Did you ever happen to notice a black truck on this road."

"You mean the truck the new guy owns? Yeah, I saw it. My guess is he was coming to scout out the place before he decided to rent it."

"No, I don't mean that truck. It's the same make and model, but there's another black truck."

"I don't know anything about that."

I can't think of anything else to ask her, so I say, "Thank you for your time. We're very sorry for the loss of your two friends."

"I just can't believe they both died." She wipes her nose with the tissue and closes the door.

Cam shoves his hands into his pockets. "Well, that explains where the Townsends were on Sunday night. Susan must have dropped them off on Main Street on her way in to work."

"Yeah, that makes sense."

"Why does it seem like Quentin isn't really investing much time in this case?" Cam asks.

"He's not. He said he's following up on my leads, but he's working another case and made it clear that was taking precedence to this one. I'm pretty sure everyone else at the BFPD still thinks it was just an accident."

"But Quentin believes you," Cam says.

"I kind of think he has to after the last case."

"Where to now?" Cam asks.

"The station. We need to find out who owns that truck."

"I'll meet you there, then. I'm just going to stop in to see how the demolition is going first."

"Good idea. I want to know, but I'm not sure I can watch after I just put so much money into fixing up the coffee shop."

"I'll handle it. Tell Quentin not to make too many stunned faces in my absence. I love watching him squirm when you one-up him."

"I'll do my best, but it's so easy to put him in his place these days."

Cam smiles and gets into his SUV.

I follow him to the end of the road where we turn in opposite directions. Then I get the weird sensation that I'm being followed. I look in my rearview window to see the black Silverado behind me. The driver has his sun visor down, so I can't fully see his face. It has to be Wes, though, right? I just came from his road. But I didn't turn toward Main Street, where Wes's office is. I went in the opposite direction.

I make a last-second decision to turn down a side street, and the truck makes the same turn. He's definitely following me. There's no way he just happened to almost miss his turn. To be sure, I pull the same trick again on the next turn. I start to overshoot it and turn at the last second. The truck turns as well.

For some reason, I don't get scared. I get angry. This guy is toying with me. He ran away from me before, and now he's following me. There's no way he has any idea who I am, so why would he act like this. I pull into the parking lot of the food store and park in the last aisle where there are no other cars. The truck pulls into the spot beside me.

I turn to look at the man's face before stepping out of my car. He clearly wants to talk to me, and I really want to talk to him, too. I slam my door, walk right over to his, and tap on his window with my knuckle.

He lowers the window. "We seem to have similar

routes this morning," he says. He looks to be in his thirties, slightly receding hairline, some gray peppering his dark sideburns.

"It's funny, though. I don't need binoculars for my morning errands. I can't help wondering why you do."

"Bird watching."

"Hmm, see I don't think so. I think you were watching a house on that road. But what I don't understand is why because you must know the people who used to live there are dead."

He leans his head back and huffs. "I suppose I should introduce myself." He raises his head to meet my gaze. "I'm Lou Kershaw. I'm a private investigator."

"You're a P.I.? What are you investigating?"

"I *was* investigating Will Townsend."

"Wait. You were following Will, not Cynthia?"

"That's correct."

"But why?"

"Because he was having an affair, with the woman whose house you just left."

I take a step back. "Hold up. Will and Susan?"

"Would you like to get in? You look a little wobbly on your feet."

"No. I'm fine." I'm not getting in this guy's truck. I want answers, but I'm not stupid. "Who hired you to follow Will?"

"I'm afraid I'm not at liberty to say. I have to respect the privacy of my clients."

"Well, I know it wasn't Cynthia, because she thought

you were following her." That poor woman was so stressed out, and she thought she was being stalked on top of everything else she was dealing with. "And you can't be a very good P.I. because Cynthia saw you on more than one occasion."

Lou snaps his gum in his mouth. "She was a jumpy one. It's awful what happened. She deserved better."

"How long had you been following Will?"

"A few weeks. I was determined to get proof of the affair."

Who would ask him to do that? One of Cynthia's friends who didn't like Will maybe? "Did you?"

"Nothing concrete, but I can tell you Will Townsend did not have a second job. He left work every day at three o'clock to go be with Susan."

"Then Susan left work at that time, too?"

"She only works until two since she's in the attendance office. She was home when Will came over. He'd park in his own driveway and walk next door. It was the perfect cover."

"But then why did people think he was working two jobs? Someone must have seen him come home."

"I'm sure they did. His supposed second job was working remotely for a rather large company I won't name. He was a customer service rep, which is hysterical if you knew him. He set up an office in the shed. That's where Cynthia thought he was late at night. Of course, he really was at…" He dips his head at me to finish his sentence.

"Susan's."

He nods. "I tried to get pictures of them together, but they were careful about it. I did overhear some interesting conversations at times, though."

"About?" I ask.

"How much Will hated his wife. How much debt she'd put them in. How he wished she'd just fall off the face of the earth so he could move on with his life."

"Because he didn't have the money to divorce her," I say.

"Bingo. You're pretty good at this."

"Okay, so he was having an affair. Why are you still watching his house if he and Cynthia are both dead?"

"I'm not. I'm watching Susan's."

I narrow my eyes at him. "Why?"

"They talked at first. Just talked. About Cynthia I mean. Then that turned into plans."

"Plans for…?" The look on his face clues me in. "I was right. He wanted to murder her in that crash."

"If only I could prove that."

"Your truck was at the same shop as the Townsends car on Sunday night."

"That's right. I followed Will there. I wanted to see what he was up to. But I had to have a reason for being there, so I asked for the simplest thing ever. A wheel alignment. I figured they'd test the alignment, say it was fine, and send me on my way. But they were closing for the night and told me to leave it for the morning. I didn't want to look suspicious, so I agreed."

"How did you get home?" I ask.

"I'm in good shape, and it's not a far walk. How would you like to help me prove that William Townsend and Susan Bell plotted Cynthia's death, only something went wrong and Will died, too?"

Something Susan kept saying plays over and over in my head. "She couldn't believe they'd both died. Both. Because Will was supposed to walk away alive."

Lou nods. "Believe me now?"

I think I do. "The police are looking into you, too. Maybe we should both go to them and tell them what you know."

"Go to whom? That Detective Peewee?"

I laugh. "It's Perry, actually."

"Not if you say it with a lisp."

I laugh again.

"See. You like me already. Come on, Coffee. What do you say?"

"You know my name?"

He tosses up both hands. "Private investigator. It's sort of my job to know things about people. And I can tell you what I know about you and Detective Perry."

Great. He knows Quentin cheated on me. I cringe as I wait for him to say as much.

"You're a much better detective than he'll ever be," Lou says.

I smirk. "You know what, Lou? I think you and I can solve this case long before Detective Peewee."

"I knew I could make that nickname stick. Hop in, Coffee."

I shake my head. "Uh-uh. I'll work with you, but I'm driving on my own."

"Suit yourself."

"I actually do have to go to the station, though. I'm meeting my boyfriend there." I don't want to tell Lou that I'm meeting Cam to get Lou's name from Quentin. He might not like that I was having the police look into him.

"I have a better idea. Tell your boyfriend to give the detective the slip and meet us at Susan Bell's place. I think there's something there you two should see."

I know how much Quentin hates private investigators, and that only makes it easier for me to say, "I'm in."

CHAPTER THIRTEEN

As soon as I get back in my car, I call Cam. "Did you go to the station yet?" I ask as soon as he answers.

"No, I'm still at Cup of Jo. The demo is going really well. The carpenter says this job is a piece of cake. He's going to match the paint in your place, not mine. That okay with you?"

"Yeah, that's fine as long as you're okay with it." I don't want Cam to feel like I'm totally taking over, even if he's already insisted that we're keeping the name Cup of Jo.

"Of course. You know me with decorating."

"Not to change the subject on you, but I have big news," I say. "Don't go to the station. Meet me at Susan Bell's house instead."

"I'm heading out now. Did Quentin find out something?" Cam asks, and I hear the beep of his SUV as he unlocks it.

"No, *I* did." He's not going to like that I met with Lou on my own when he could have been the killer, and I don't want him driving angry, so I say, "I'll tell you everything when we get there."

"I know that's Jo speak for 'I did something you're not going to like.'"

"You always did know me best. See you in a few." I end the call before he can ask any more questions. I'm following Lou since I don't know what it is exactly that he wants to show me, and I'm assuming he doesn't want Susan Bell to see us. He parks at the opposite end of the street and gets out of the truck. I pull up next to him and meet him around the front of our vehicles. He has his binoculars in hand.

"Your guy on his way?" he asks me.

"Should be here any minute. What exactly is it that you want to show me?"

He takes a pack of cinnamon gum out of his pocket, spits his old gum onto the road, and pops a new piece into his mouth before offering the pack to me. I shake my head, so he repockets it. "I don't expect you to take my word on anything since you don't know me. I'm going to show you how I know Will and Susan were having an affair."

"You really don't have any pictures of them together?" I ask.

"Would you really want to see them if I did?"

Ew. No. I shake my head again.

"I have something better than pictures. I'm going to

walk you through how Will would sneak out of the shed and over to Susan's without Cynthia knowing."

"That doesn't exactly prove he did it, though." Like he said, I'm not just going to take his word for it without proof.

Cam's SUV comes into view, and I swear I can feel the panic emanating from him when he pulls up to the black Silverado. He parks next to me and rushes out. "What is going on?"

"Cam, it's okay. This is Lou Kershaw. He's a private investigator. He was following Will Townsend because Will was having an affair with Susan Bell. He believes Will and Susan planned the accident to kill Cynthia, but something went wrong and Will died, too." I blurt it all out as quickly as I can. "Lou is going to help us figure out what really happened."

Cam looks shocked, and he steps closer to me as if he doesn't trust Lou. "You're a P.I.? Who hired you to look into Will?"

"I can't tell you that. It's a confidentiality thing."

"Well, we know it wasn't Cynthia since she clearly thought you were stalking her," Cam says.

"No, it wasn't Cynthia. I can tell you that much." Lou motions toward Susan's house. "Why don't you let me show you what I've discovered? Then you can decide if you think I'm telling the truth."

Cam nods and motions for Lou to lead the way. "Do you really think this guy is who he says he is?" he whispers to me.

"It makes sense, doesn't it? I mean Cynthia was stalked in high school and totally stressed about her mother's health and their empty bank account. I can see how she'd think she was being stalked when Lou was really watching Will."

Cam nods. "I suppose so. What about the plot to kill Cynthia?"

"I've thought Will might have resented Cynthia and wanted to kill her for a while. No one I've talked to has really had a good word to say about Will, only Cynthia. That could mean he wasn't friendly or even a good person at all."

"Do you think one of Cynthia's friends might have hired Lou?" Cam asks. "You know, to try to help Cynthia get away from Will?"

"Maybe, but neither could afford to go through a divorce. They were broke. So I'm not sure proving an affair would have helped Cynthia unless the end goal was to just get Cynthia to walk away from him. But where would she go?"

"If you're wondering if Cynthia was also having an affair, the answer is no," Lou says. "Sorry. I didn't mean to eavesdrop. I just happen to have exceptional hearing. It comes in handy in my line of work."

"I imagine it does," I say.

We come to Wes's house, and his truck is gone, so I know he's at work by now. We walk into his backyard.

"Like I told you, Coffee, Will had an office in the shed. At least, that's what he called it. Really, it's a couch and a TV, but Cynthia didn't know that. Not that it mattered anyway. This place was just an alibi for when he was with Susan." Lou walks over to the shed, which is locked. He turns to look at Cam and me. "Neither of you is a cop, right?"

"No," I say.

"Good, then you won't have a problem with me doing this." He pulls out a lockpick kit from his jacket pocket.

"You know anything you find in there can't be used against Will since you're technically breaking in," I say.

"I'm not planning to use anything as evidence for the police. I'm only trying to convince you two." He gets the lock open and removes it before putting the kit back into his pocket. He opens the shed to show us an ugly brown couch that has clearly seen better days. There are some tools hanging from hooks on a pegboard on the left wall. Underneath is a shelf. And sitting on top of that shelf is a tool belt. An empty tool belt. I walk over to it, and Cam follows.

"You don't think…" is all Cam manages to say.

"That Will might be Tool all grown up?" I ask. Another thought hits me, nearly knocking me over. "Wait. Will packed up all his things. This stuff must belong to Wes."

"What did you say?" Lou asks us.

I turn to face him. "When Cynthia was in high school, she was stalked by this kid. She didn't know his real name because everyone just called him Tool."

"Because he wore an empty tool belt all the time," Cam clarifies.

"Like this one. But this isn't Will's stuff. It's Wes's," I say.

Lou shakes his head. "I know for a fact that Will left the tools in this shed. He wasn't taking them with him. He only packed his clothing when they moved out of the house. The house was still fully furnished, too, when that Wes guy moved in."

I breathe a sigh of relief. "Then that means Will could be that kid from high school. What if he continued to stalk Cynthia and wound up marrying her?"

Lou bobs his head. "I suppose that's possible, but wouldn't someone in town recognize him if he never left?"

"Who's to say he didn't?" I ask. "He could have left, changed his name, and come back." Will Townsend wasn't one of the students listed in the "No Photo" section of the junior class in the 2003 yearbook. "We don't know if Will went to high school here. We never checked."

"You can access most yearbooks online nowadays," Lou says. "It's easy enough." He pulls out his phone. "You said 2003, right?"

"Yeah. That guy that stalked Cynthia was a year younger than she was. That was Cynthia's senior year, so he would have been a junior."

"I'm going to search Will's name. It will show me where he is in the yearbook," Lou says. He stops typing and furrows his brow. "He wasn't in the yearbook at all. He couldn't have gone to high school here in Bennett Falls."

"Unless I'm right and he did change his name." I turn back to the tool belt. It's definitely not the same one. It's not old enough to be. But the fact that it's sitting empty strikes me as odd.

"Why don't I keep showing you what I found?" Lou suggests.

I nod.

"Okay, so the shed has a back door. Odd, right? I mean who needs two doors on a shed, unless they're sneaking out the back?" Lou says, opening the back door of the shed.

"All right, I'll give you the fact that it's odd, but it still doesn't prove anything."

"This is where it gets a little trickier since Susan is home," Lou says. He points to the shed in Susan's backyard. "Notice they're identical."

"Maybe there was a sale on that particular style," Cam says.

"Or maybe they bought them at the same time." Lou holds up his hands. "I know. No proof. But check this out." He uses the binoculars, which have been in his back jeans pocket, to look at Susan's house. "She isn't in the kitchen or the upstairs bedroom, so she shouldn't be able to see us. Let's go." He quickly makes his way to her shed. I expect him to take out his lockpick kit again, but instead he reaches for the doorknob and opens it. "It's never locked," he tells us. "She keeps it open so Will can easily slip inside." He steps aside, letting us go into the shed first.

There are no tools in this shed. It looks like a second living room. "It's a she shed," I say.

"With a couch that pulls out into a bed." Lou grabs the bottom of the couch and opens it to reveal a queen-size mattress. "This is why I couldn't get pictures of them together. Notice the lack of windows in the shed. When those two were together, they were here, and I couldn't see inside."

"Okay, so maybe they were having an affair. How do we prove they were plotting Cynthia's death?" I ask.

"Susan invited Cynthia and Will to stay here their last night in town, right?" Lou says.

"Yeah. She told us as much."

"When Cynthia fell asleep, Will and Susan came out here. They talked about the plan."

"Did you record it?" Cam asks.

Lou smiles. "I did. I missed some of it, but I caught enough." He pulls out his phone once again and brings up the recording. He hits play.

"Your car is going in because of a problem with the brakes. You can claim they didn't fix them properly," Susan says.

"And with all the water on Second Street, I can claim I slid. I just have to hit the building on the passenger side. She'll die, and I'll be free of her debt and left to collect the life insurance. She's got enough years in working at the school that her policy will yield a nice chunk of change."

"Then we'll keep our relationship on the down low until enough time has passed that people won't suspect anything. I mean it's only normal that Cynthia's husband and friend would console each other after her unfortunate death." Susan laughs.

"That's it," Lou says, turning off the recording.

"That's plenty. You have to take this to Detective Perry. It's all there. Premeditated murder." I can't believe this. We can wrap up the case today.

"Or we can get a confession out of her," Lou says. "That's always more fun. Plus, it keeps me from getting involved. Cops don't really care for me butting in on their investigations. I'd rather keep my name out of it."

"You want me to run with this information and get a confession," I say.

"I'd prefer it, yes. I'm trying to honor my client's right to privacy. If I go to the police with this, they're going to ask me a lot of questions about why I was there in the first place."

"I don't suppose you want to give me that recording either, then," I say.

"Sorry, Coffee. You're on your own from here. It's time for me to move on to another case. I've gotta pay the bills, too."

"You're leaving town?' I ask.

"Yup. I already have the next case lined up. I'm sure I'm leaving this in capable hands." He smiles and nods to me before walking out of the shed.

"He's an odd guy," Cam says.

"I won't argue there, but he is a good P.I."

"Do we call Quentin now and get him here to question Susan?"

"Yeah, I think—"

The front door of the shed opens, and Susan Bell points a gun right at us.

CHAPTER FOURTEEN

"Easy there," Cam says, holding up his hands in front of him. "Don't shoot."

"What are you doing in my shed?" Susan asks. "This is private property."

"Ms. Bell, we'd just like to talk to you," I say.

She sees the open bed, and her eyes narrow on us. "You think you figured it out, don't you?"

"That you were having an affair with Will Townsend?" I ask. "Yeah, we know."

She almost looks relieved, and I can't help wondering if it's because she thinks that's all we know. I decide to play up the sympathy card.

"I don't blame you and Will. I'm sure he was under a lot of stress."

"Stress she caused. She spent every dime they had."

"I know. I can't even imagine how awful that must

have been for him. And you were such a good friend to stand by him. It's only natural that he would seek comfort in you."

She lowers the gun. "Cynthia was a terrible wife. Will deserved so much better. I'm really not sure why he married her in the first place. It was clear their marriage was over. He told me as much, too."

I nod. "Cynthia's friends hinted at that, too," I lie as I try to come up with some reason to get Quentin here that won't totally set Susan off and make her use that gun after all.

"Why are you here?" she asks us.

My mind begins to spin, trying to concoct a believable story. "One of Cynthia's friends said Cynthia had a secret stash of money. She mentioned it was in the shed. We checked her old shed, but it wasn't there. So we thought maybe she hid it in yours to keep Will from finding it."

Cam picks up on what I'm doing. "Yeah, with his office in his shed it was too risky putting it there, but she never thought he'd think to look in here."

"She hid money in here? Money she kept from Will?" Susan is completely outraged. "If it's here, it's legally mine. Possession is nine-tenths of the law, right?"

"Right," I say.

"And you two were searching for it so you could steal it." She raises the gun again.

"No," I blurt out. "I was investigating the accident,

and I discovered Cynthia was hiding money from Will. I'm just trying to find it to prove that. I know we should have told you first, but you were so upset about Will's death."

"I want you out of here. I'll call the cops. You're trespassing, and that money is mine."

Please call the police! I raise my hands. "I understand if you want to press charges. We did trespass."

"Are you saying you want me to turn you in?" she asks.

"I don't want you to shoot us, so if the alternative is having us arrested, then go ahead."

Cam nods.

Susan considers her options. "I don't plan to go to jail for shooting you both, but I am outnumbered and there's money here. I think I will call the cops."

I nod. "Detective Perry has it out for me, so maybe ask for someone else," I say.

Cam gives me the side-eye, wondering what I'm up to.

"I want to make sure you two don't come back here now that you know I have this money," Susan says. She keeps the gun trained in our direction and pulls her phone out of her back pocket to make the call. She presses four buttons, which I assume are 9-1-1 and the call button. "I need Detective Perry with the Bennett Falls PD."

I do my best to look upset. Luckily, Cam pulls off the

act much better because I'm not sure I would have convinced Susan.

"I caught two trespassers in my shed. I'd like to press charges." She pauses. "I can hold them until you get here."

She gets off the phone and motions the nose of the gun toward the bed. "Sit down."

As much as I don't want to sit on that bed, I don't have a choice. I sit on the very edge, and Cam sits so close we're pressed up against each other.

"Don't move. The police will be here in a few minutes." She keeps the gun on us while she looks around the shed. "Any idea where that money might be?"

"Not really." I can't exactly lead her to money that doesn't exist.

"Well, you better hope I find it, or I'll be charging you with theft as well."

Since she has no idea how much money it's supposed to be and we have none on us, she'll never make that charge stick. She opens the drawers on the apothecary table and searches each one.

I hear the sirens of Quentin's car outside, and Susan pokes her head out the door. "In here, Detective," she calls before focusing on us again.

As soon as Quentin reaches the shed, he asks her to lower her gun. "What exactly is going on here?" His gaze immediately goes to me.

"These two broke into my shed to try to steal money from me," Susan says.

"Actually, we didn't break in. The door was unlocked, the way you always left it so William Townsend could sneak in here to be with you. And we didn't come looking for money. I lied about that. We came to prove that you and Will plotted that accident to kill Cynthia so he'd be free of her and her debt."

Susan starts to raise her gun hand, but Quentin immediately strips the weapon from her. He puts it in the waistband of his pants and turns to her. "Care to tell me what Joanna is talking about?"

"You set me up," she says to me. "You wanted me to call him specifically. But why? Didn't I hear he cheated on you?"

"Yeah, he did, which means you two should get along well since you're both cheaters. But Quentin is also the detective looking into the Townsend murder."

"You knew it was murder?" she says and realizes her slip too late. "I mean, what makes you think that's what it was?"

"You tipped me off, actually." I stand up now that she's unarmed. "You were so distraught about the news of their deaths, and you kept telling me you couldn't believe they'd both died. *Both* being the key word. You and Will planned to stage an accident. He was going to 'lose control'"—I make air quotes—"of the car due to the water on the ground and hit the building on the passenger side. But something went wrong, and he really did lose control."

Susan starts sobbing. "It was awful. I saw the entire thing."

"Because the Townsends stayed here Sunday night. You drove them to Main Street, claiming it was easy to drop them off on your way to work. But you never went to work that day, did you?"

She shakes her head. "I couldn't after that. It was horrible."

"You stuck around because you wanted to see Cynthia was dead. Maybe you wanted to console your good friend Will, too. Maybe offer him a place to stay since he was kicked out of his house? What then? Did you two plan to wait a while so people didn't get suspicious about your relationship?" I already know that's true, but without Lou's recording, I need Susan to admit to it in front of Quentin.

Susan wipes her nose with the back of her sleeve. "It wouldn't be strange for us to seek comfort in each other after Will lost his wife and I lost my friend."

"No, but Cynthia was never your friend. You only pretended to be her friend so she wouldn't suspect you were sleeping with her husband," I say.

"She didn't love him. All she cared about was her mother. The debt was killing him, and she didn't even notice." Susan is screaming now. "I was there for him when no one else was."

"And you helped him plan to get rid of her," I say, needing her to confirm as much.

"I would have done anything for him."

"So you helped him figure out how to kill her." Just admit it already!

"Yes, I helped him. I never thought he'd get hurt. He said he could do it. That he was a great driver, and it would be easy. Then we'd collect her life insurance, and everything would be good. We could start our life together."

Quentin holsters his gun and pulls out his handcuffs. "Ms. Bell, I need you to put your hands behind your back." He takes her arm and helps her into the position before cuffing her. He reads her rights, but I'm not sure she hears a single word because she's sobbing Will's name.

We follow Quentin to his patrol car, where he gets her into the back seat. "I have so many things to say to you, Jo." His jaw is clenched.

"Why do I think none of them contains the words *thank you*?"

"This isn't a joke. You were trespassing. You could have been killed."

"I'm well aware."

"How did you even get to this point? How did you figure out she and Will devised this plan?"

I'm not about to throw Lou under the bus after he helped me solve the case. "What can I say? I missed my calling. That or all the coffee I drink gives me superpowers."

"This conversation isn't over. I'm going to book her, but then you and I will be having more words."

Having words. He always said that when we were dating and he was upset with me. "We're going to have words about this, Jo." I might hate it even more now.

"Sorry, Detective, but I have plans this evening. It's the grand opening of S.C. Tunney's. Rain check, though." I start walking toward my car.

"As much as I hate that guy, you really do need to be careful what you say to him," Cam says. "He could charge us with trespassing."

"He won't. I mean could you imagine the buzz that would create around town. He's already disliked for hurting me." Most people seem to have excused Samantha since she's oblivious to her wrongdoings, but Quentin's reputation took a hit.

"I guess this case is closed then. It was premeditated murder gone wrong."

"Case closed. Now it's time to celebrate."

Even though Mo asked Wes to the grand opening and we drove separately, we get a table together. Lance reserved the back corner table for us. The restaurant looks absolutely breathtaking. There's a gigantic fish tank built into the wall that separates the dining room from the kitchen. The lighting is very dim, giving the place a very romantic vibe and making me wish we weren't sharing a table with my little sister and the guy she just started dating. All the tables are covered in black linens with tiny tea lights floating in mini bowl-shaped glass vases in the center of the table.

Instead of a waiter coming to greet us, Lance comes out, dressed head to toe in black. "Welcome to S.C. Tunney's" he says.

"Lance, this place looks incredible," I say, getting up to give him a hug. When I pull away, I add, "And so do you. I love the new look."

"All thanks to you. I'll never be able to repay you for that inheritance check you gave me." Even in the dim lighting, I can see his eyes watering.

"Mr. Cromwell believed in you, and so do I. This place is going to be a huge success. I can't think of a better use for that money."

Lance swipes a tear that escapes his right eye. "Well, your meals are always on the house."

"Um, the rest of us are paying, though," Cam says. "Let's just get that straight right now. I know you and Jo worked out a barter system, but the three of us are paying customers."

"If you insist," Lance says. "I have to go greet some more customers, but if you need anything, let me know. Enjoy your meal."

"I know we will." I squeeze his hand before retaking my seat.

"He's such a sweet guy," Mo says. "I'm glad I helped him with those ads for free."

Wes reaches for Mo's hand and raises it to kiss the

back. "And I think you're really sweet for helping him like that."

These two look like they've been together for months, not days. I'm not sure how I feel about that. I want Mo to be happy, but I don't want her to rush into anything. We still don't know much about Wes.

"I heard you had a hand in arresting my neighbor today," Wes says.

"Yeah, about that, I guess in the name of full disclosure, I should tell you we were also in your shed today. Sorry."

Wes laughs. "That's okay. I actually haven't even gone in there yet. The previous owners left some tools and such, according to the landlord."

Tools. I forgot about the tool belt. I was way off base with suspecting that kid from Cynthia's high school. She probably just felt like she was experiencing déjà vu when she thought she was being followed. Little did she know Lou was actually trailing Will. Still, it would have been really interesting if Will had turned out to be Tool. But life isn't a murder mystery.

"I still can't believe you two solved the case," Mo says.

"Well, to be honest, we had some help from a P.I. looking into Will. He was the one who owned the black truck."

"Oh, the one that made you suspect Wes," Mo says, completely shocking me.

Wes laughs again. "Don't look so embarrassed, Jo. I

don't blame you for being careful with Mo. I understand the desire to protect the people you love."

"Thanks for understanding. And I have to say, you might be my favorite of the guys Mo's dated."

"You make it sound like I date a lot," Mo says.

"No, you're actually really picky."

"A lot pickier than you are," she says. "Speaking of, look who just walked in."

Quentin and Samantha are at the hostess station, Samantha's arm laced through his.

"Great. Sometimes I think this town is way too small." Though in truth, S.C. Tunney's is twenty minutes outside of Bennett Falls.

The waiter comes to take our drink order, and when he turns to walk away, he almost walks smack into Quentin and Samantha.

"Detective," I say. "No need to thank me for solving that case for you."

"I wasn't going to because the case isn't solved."

"What are you talking about? I got you a confession. What more do you want?"

"How about an explanation for who drained the brake fluid from the car? Or did you forget about that detail?" He steps closer to the table. "See, this is the problem with amateurs thinking they can play detective. My job's a lot harder than it looks. You can't dismiss things you can't explain. Will and Susan might have planned to murder Cynthia, but the fact that Will lost control of the vehicle had nothing to do with a slippery road. It had everything to do with someone trying to kill him."

I'm completely speechless because he's right. The case isn't over. Someone tried to kill Will Townsend, and we still have no idea who that someone is.

CHAPTER FIFTEEN

Cam laces his fingers through mine under the table, but I still can't speak.

"This is why you should have told Quentin what you knew, Jo," Samantha says. "You shouldn't go behind people's backs like that. It's just rude, and it makes you look stupid in the end."

Okay, that does it. I find my will to speak again. "You're right, Samantha. Going behind someone's back is an awful thing to do."

"Jo," Quentin says in a warning tone, but I'm not about to stop. I've held this in for way too long.

"No, she needs to hear this," I say, letting go of Cam's hand and getting to my feet. "You were supposed to be my best friend. I took you under my wing when everyone else laughed and made fun of you. And you had the audacity to stab me in the back by sleeping with my boyfriend. You want to talk about rude? It doesn't get any ruder than that. You committed the ultimate betrayal, and you've never acknowledged it. No sorry for being the worst best friend in the history of friends. No begging me to forgive you for being a cheating..." I swallow the word I want to call her. "You act like I should still call you my best friend. Like you did absolutely nothing wrong. So if you want to talk about people looking stupid, you should turn to your fiancé, and the both of you should stand in front of a full-length mirror to take in what truly awful human beings look like."

Everyone in the restaurant is staring at me, and I realize I've been screaming. I swallow hard again and rush toward the bathrooms in the back.

Mo hurries after me. "Jo." She grabs my arm to stop me from locking myself in a stall. "Are you okay?"

"I didn't mean to say all that. I just couldn't take it anymore. Her comments and her judgements. She has no right to judge me when she..."

Mo wraps her arms around me. "I know. Everyone in town knows. They're both total fart brains."

I pull away and laugh at her use of the phrase she equated to cursing when we were kids. "Thanks. I need to laugh."

"I know." She rubs my arms.

"I feel like such a jerk for blowing up like that in Lance's restaurant. God, I'm no better than Samantha and Quentin."

"Don't ever say that."

Someone knocks on the door, which is odd since this

isn't a single bathroom, but being that it's opening day, maybe this person doesn't know that. "Come in," I say.

To my surprise, it's Lance.

"You don't have to kick me out. I'll go. I'm so sorry I made a scene at your grand opening."

"Kick you out? Why would I do that?" Lance shakes his head. "Those two had it coming if you ask me. They're the ones I asked to leave."

"You didn't have to do that. They were paying customers."

"I don't want customers like them. Besides, you're my friend, or at least, I hope you are."

"Of course, we're friends," I say.

"Good. Then go enjoy your meal."

"I'm not sure I can go back out there. I made such a scene."

"You didn't say anything everyone else here wasn't already thinking. In fact, the only talk I've heard is how people are proud of you for standing up to them."

"Seriously?" I ask.

He nods. "I wouldn't be surprised if you go back in there and get a standing ovation."

I laugh. "Thanks, Lance."

"Go eat." He gives my arm a gentle squeeze before walking out.

"See. It's all okay," Mo says.

I look at myself in the mirror and use my finger to fix my smudged eye liner. "You know, there was a part of me that wondered if you and Lance would wind up dating."

"Oh, he's adorable and totally sweet. But I'm not looking to find someone serious right now, and I'd never want to hurt him."

I turn to face her. "But you and Wes look like you've been together for a while. Why are you seeing him so much if you don't want something serious?"

"I didn't mean for that to happen. I guess I didn't think we'd click like this."

The bathroom door opens, and Samantha walks in.

"I thought you were asked to leave," Mo says, stepping between Samantha and me.

"I wanted to talk to Jo first." She tilts her head to see me better. "I didn't know you were mad at me. You didn't act mad. And I sort of figured you and Cam were meant to be the way Quentin and I are. Everything worked out for the best, you know?"

"That's not for you to decide," Mo says, crossing her arms.

"Mo." I place my hand on her shoulder, and she steps aside. "Samantha, I don't doubt things worked out for the best, but I lost a lot of respect for you and Quentin. You both should have talked to me before you started seeing each other. But you chose to ruin our relationships instead. Nothing's going to change that now. We aren't friends. We'll never be friends again. You're welcome to come to Cup of Jo still. I'll serve you and I'll be cordial, but that's all I'm willing to offer you." I start to walk out, and she calls after me.

"Jo, I'm sorry. I screwed up."

I turn to face her. "Yeah, you did. Thanks for finally admitting it." I walk out.

Mo loops her arm through mine, and we walk right past Quentin back to our table.

Saturday morning, Cam and I check in on Cup of Jo. The wall is down and the debris from the demolition has been cleared away.

"Today we spackle," Ben, the contractor, tells us. "This is the slow part of the process because it's going to take three coats, and we need each coat to fully dry before putting on the next one."

"Still, this is moving along really quickly," I say.

"Glad you think so. We're used to working quickly because most business owners are breathing down our necks so they can reopen."

"You're doing great. Really. And Cam says you're good with the paint color."

"Yeah, we'll grab the paint today so we'll have it once we've spackled and sanded. The only other question is do you want to keep two separate counters if this is going to be one place? I can make you a longer one if you'd like. I have a guy on the crew who makes custom counters. He can take the dimensions and make it match the style you currently have."

"How much will that run us?" I ask.

Ben scrunches his face. "Tell you what. You give me those two counters, and we'll call it even."

"We're bartering?" I ask.

"I only barter with locals. Besides, if I'm being honest, I can use these two on other jobs. They're practically brand new."

That's true. Cam's Kitchen was only open for a few days, and Cup of Jo has been open for a month. "You've got yourself a deal, Ben." I extend my hand, and he shakes it.

"We'll keep you posted on the progress then."

"Thanks."

Cam and I walk out onto Main Street.

"What do you want to do today?" he asks.

What I really want to do is finish solving this case. It's bothering me that Quentin was right. I overlooked a key detail because it was convenient to charge Susan with premeditated murder. But someone else had a part in this, and she might know who.

"I want to go talk to Susan Bell."

Cam cocks his head at me. "She's being held at the station. You know you'd have to go through Quentin to see her."

"I know." One thing I've learned is I can't avoid my past.

"I'll go with you, then."

I knew he would. He drives us to the station and holds my hand as we walk in. Quentin raises his eyes to us but continues to work. I'm sure the entire station is aware of what happened at S.C. Tunney's last night. Before I went inside Cup of Jo this morning, a few people walking along Main Street stopped to congratulate me for putting Samantha and Quentin in their place. I walk up to Quentin's desk. "I want to talk to Susan Bell."

"No." He continues tapping away on his keyboard, only using two fingers because he's the worst typist in the world.

I take a deep breath. "You were right about something last night. This case isn't over. Susan might know something that can tell us who tampered with Will's car."

"Then I'll find that out. You are officially done working cases with the BFPD."

"I was never working cases with the BFPD. Not in an official capacity. Or did I somehow miss my consulting checks?" I sit down. "You know you need me. You can complain about my methods, but I do get results." I'm tempted to tell him people in this town are much more likely to open up to me than him, but I know I'm already pushing my luck.

"Go home, Jo. Stick to what you're good at, selling coffee."

"That's how it's going to be then? You really want me to make you look bad? Again? Because I'm going to solve this case. I know something you don't, and without that information, you're not going to find your killer." I'm starting to think the person who hired Lou might have wanted Will dead. Lou might have inadvertently provided the killer with the information he needed to murder Will.

"You have two choices. Go home, or I can go talk to Susan Bell myself and see if she'd like me to press trespassing charges against the two of you."

"Why don't we go ask her together?" I say, calling his bluff.

He stands up. "Let's go."

Does he realize he's giving me what I came here for? He must actually think she'll press charges, but I have a feeling she'll be more interested in helping me than charging me with anything.

Quentin brings us downstairs to Susan's holding cell. She sits up on the bed when she sees us.

"What are you two doing here?"

"We came to help you," I say.

Susan laughs, but it quickly turns to sobs. "You put me in here. Haven't you done enough? I've already lost everything. Unless you can bring Will back, I don't want to talk to you."

"I can't do that, but I can find out who is responsible for his death."

"He lost control of the car. It was an accident," she says.

I step closer to the bars. "No, it wasn't. Someone drained the brake fluid after Will had the new brakes put in."

"It wasn't Will's fault?"

"Why would you think it was his fault?" I ask.

She laces her fingers in her lap. "I suppose it doesn't matter now if I tell you. You already know he was trying to kill Cynthia."

"Tell us what you know, and help us catch the person who is responsible for Will's death, Susan."

Quentin tilts his head back, and I know he can't believe I'm pulling this off.

"He had to speed out of the car shop so it would really look like he hydroplaned or whatever on Second Street."

"And you thought it was because he was speeding that he lost control for real," I say.

She nods. "But he couldn't have used his brakes?"

"No. He couldn't."

"Who would do that?"

"I was hoping you might have some idea."

"Why?"

"I'm guessing he confided in you more than his wife."

"He loved me."

"I know. So think. Did he ever mention fighting with anyone?"

"His landlord."

Rudy Wilcox needs a cane to get around. I don't see him sneaking into the car shop after hours and tampering with Will's car, but I don't want to discourage Susan, so I say, "Okay, good. Anyone else? We want to look into every possibility so we catch the right person."

"Well, I don't know if this helps because Will never

knew who did it, but they'd get calls on the landline. The person wouldn't talk, but Will heard them breathing. And at work once, someone mailed him an empty tool belt. There was no return address or anything. Will teaches biology, so he had no idea why anyone would send him a tool belt. Cynthia was pretty freaked out by it, though. She even told him she wanted to move after that, but Will wouldn't leave me."

Cam and I share a look.

"The tool belt in Will's shed?" I ask. "Is that the one?"

She nods. "That's the one."

Is that proof that someone figured out Will is Tool from high school? Or did Tool find Cynthia and the tool belt was a threat to Will's life?

CHAPTER SIXTEEN

When we leave Susan, Quentin calls after us.

"I know you know something, Jo." His gaze volleys between us. "You both do. Tell me what it is."

I'm not willing to tell Quentin everything, but I could use his help figuring out if Will Townsend used to be called Tool. "Can we talk in private?" I ask him.

He brings us to his desk and motions for us to sit. "Now spill it."

"There's a possibility Will Townsend is the guy who used to stalk Cynthia in high school."

"How so? Will moved here after he graduated college. That's when he was hired at the school," Quentin says.

"It's normal for people to leave town to go to college. You and I both did," I say. "What if he came back using a different name?"

"Then his teaching certificate would be a fake," Quentin says.

"Unless he went to college under the fake name," Cam offers. "He could have changed his name after leaving Bennett Falls."

"That's true," I say. "Then his teaching certificate would be legitimate."

"Only if he legally changed his name," Quentin says. "I can do some digging to find out."

"Do that."

Quentin gives me a look. "This is my case, Jo. You don't get to boss me around."

I'd do it myself if I had the resources, but I don't. I tap my foot impatiently.

"This is going to take a little bit. I need to verify the teaching license and Townsend's transcripts. Everything really. You two might as well go."

"Because you'll call us to let us know what you find out?" I ask. More like he'll find out and we'll hear about it on the news when he cracks the case.

"Bye, Jo," Quentin says.

The man is so infuriating, but I have someone else who can get the information for me. A private detective who I happened to know is good at his job. I smile at Quentin, letting him know I have more tricks up my sleeve, and walk out.

"What do you know, Jo?" Quentin calls after me, but I just raise a hand and wiggle my fingers in the air as we step outside.

Cam starts the car and pulls out of the lot. "Are we going to see Mo?"

"Yup. I need her to help me find Lou. We have to know who hired him to follow Will, and he'll also be able to help us figure out if Will is Tool."

Cam looks at me briefly. "Let me get this straight. You're going to hire a P.I. to solve this crime before Quentin?"

"Yup. The look on Quentin's face will be totally worth the money."

At Mo's office, she searches for more about William Townsend first, but it's too common of a name. She can't weed through what's him and what's not. "Sorry, Jo."

"It's okay. I just need to get in touch with Lou then. I don't have his number, but he must be listed since he runs a P.I. company."

"Do you know the name of it?" she asks me, fingers poised over the keyboard.

"No. Is that a problem?"

"Not necessarily. What state does he work out of?"

I shrug. "All I know is his name. Lou Kershaw."

"Okay." She draws out the word, not giving me much hope she believes that's enough to go on.

"I know I'm asking for miracles, but I have complete faith in you," I say.

"As nice as that is to hear, it doesn't help me one iota in this search."

"Okay, you do your thing. I'm going to head to the bed and breakfast and see if he was staying there. If he was, he must have left a number or address with Elena Reede when he checked in."

"Good thinking. I'll call if I get anything."

Cam and I drive to the B&B. I'm not sure Elena will be happy to see us again after I thought her mother's pills were murder weapons in a previous case. Oops. It was an honest mistake, and I totally cleared Mary Ellen's name. Not that anyone thought the eighty-two-year-old woman would commit murder.

We walk inside to see Elena at her usual post at the check-in desk. Her entire body stiffens when she spots us.

"Please tell me this has nothing to do with a police investigation," she says when we approach her.

"I wish I could, but we need to know if someone by the name of Lou Kershaw was staying here."

She shakes her head. "No, I didn't check in anyone by that name."

"Could you double check, please?" I ask.

She rolls her eyes, but she flips through the book in front of her. "Nope. Sorry. Looks like you can't tie my B&B to any investigations this time."

"Are you still looking to find someone to buy out your share of the place?" I ask her.

"No, I've resigned myself to working here until Mother passes. Then I'll sell it."

"I see. Well, that's very nice of you to stay here while she's alive. I know how much it means to her. How is she doing?"

"She's old. Her body is giving out on her, but her mind is as sharp as ever."

"Please tell her we said hello."

"I will."

Cam's phone rings as we head out of the B&B. "It's Ben, the carpenter," he tells me before answering the call. "Hello? Yeah, we can come there. We'll leave now." He pockets the phone. "Ben got an idea to put in a window in the wall between the kitchen and the area where you'll be taking orders. He thinks it will help us communicate and keep you from having to run back into the kitchen every time someone places an order for a baked good. He wants to run it by us."

"Okay, let's go. It doesn't sound like a bad idea." I get in and click my seat belt into place.

"I'm not sure I'll be doing all that much baking to order, though, so it might be an added expense we don't need. It would also add on time to the remodel and delay reopening."

"Probably not by too much if they do it before the spackling and painting gets done. Besides, it will be nice to be able to see each other when you're in the kitchen and I'm upfront."

He reaches for my hand. "You might have sold me on the idea right there."

Twenty minutes later, we're in agreement about the window. Ben takes measurements to make sure the placement of the window won't interfere with my coffee machines. He tries to upsell us on moving the doorway so there's only one and it's in the center, but we nix that idea immediately. I like having two doorways. It will give our place character and make us different from all the other shops on the strip.

"If you have this under control here, I'm going to run across the street and see if Mo was able to come up with anything," I tell Cam.

"Okay, yeah. I'm good. Meet me back here when you're done?"

"You got it," I say. "Keep up the good work, boys!" I call to the crew on my way out. I should probably bring a large coffee urn for them tomorrow morning. And maybe Cam should bake some scones or muffins. They are doing a great job expediting this remodel. It only seems right to do something nice for them in return.

I'm walking across the street when I spot a familiar face out of the corner of my eye. "Lou!" I wave and jog over to him at the intersection of Main and Second Street. "I've been looking for you. I thought you left town."

"That was the plan, but I had to settle the bill with my client first." He spits out his gum, missing the garbage can completely. He doesn't seem to notice since he makes no move to pick up the gum.

"Speaking of your client, are you sure I can't convince you to tell me who that is?"

"Why do you want to know?" He pops a new piece of cinnamon gum into his mouth, once again offering the pack to me.

"No, thank you. It's just that Quentin is convinced the case isn't closed. He says someone definitely tampered with Will's car. I need to find out who hated Will enough to want him dead."

"Ah." Lou bobs his head. "And you thought my client might be that someone."

"You have to admit it makes sense. Your client knew the kind of man Will really was."

"I won't argue with you there."

"But?"

"But I'm not telling you my client's name. Sorry, Coffee."

"Okay, then I'd like to hire you to find out who drained the brake fluid from Will Townsend's car."

He puts his hands in his pockets. "You're serious, aren't you?"

"I am. Truth be told, the detective working the case is my ex, and I'd like to show him up."

Lou laughs. "I like you, Coffee."

"Does that mean you'll help me out?"

"I suppose I can hang around for a little while longer."

"What about the other case you mentioned?"

He takes a minute to think about it. "Tell you what. Let me make a phone call. Can I meet you in say an hour?"

"Sure. How about at Cup of Jo. It's closed for renovations, but you can come right inside."

"Sounds good."

"Great!" I turn back toward Mo's office, ready to tell her she can stop looking for Lou when I realize I should get his number in case I need to get in touch with him again. When I turn back around, he's gone. Where did he go?

I peer into the waiting area in the car shop, but he's not inside. Did he go down Second Street? It's still barricaded since the drainage system needs to be repaired, but people can easily ignore the barricade and walk down it. Maybe he did just that so he'd have privacy for his phone call.

I walk toward Second Street to see. The sidewalk is empty. Lou must have had his truck parked on Main Street and I just didn't notice it. He probably drove away when I turned my back. I shake my head at myself for being so unobservant when I notice Cam's old kitchen. It still makes me sad that it was destroyed.

I pull out my phone and text Mo that she can stop looking for Lou because I found him. Then I walk to the old space. The police tape is still across it, but I get a lot of satisfaction in ignoring anything Quentin does or says, so I carefully duck under it and walk inside. There's rubble everywhere. Cam's old stove is dented in, and the door is hanging by one hinge, the glass in the front completely shattered. I'm just glad he'd already moved to the new location before the crash. Still, this place holds a lot of memories. Like walking in to find Cam in his grandmother's lace apron. I smile and step toward the large island where Cam prepared the foods before putting them in the oven. I have to be careful to step over all the debris. If I twist an ankle in here and have to call for help, I'll be caught trespassing for the second time in two days. Quentin would probably love to fine me or make me spend some time behind bars right now.

I step over a broken brick, and my boot sticks to the floor. Ew. I lift my foot to see I've stepped in gum. "Who would leave gum on the floor like this?" Three things hit me at the same time. First, Cam doesn't chew gum, so this wasn't his doing. Second, this gum is fresh considering how gooey it is, stretching from the floor to my raised boot. And third, it's cinnamon gum. I can smell it.

This space has been empty since Cam moved out of it, making it the perfect place for someone to hide, and now I know who that someone is. The person I've been looking for from the start, only I didn't know it was him when I found him.

"Oh, God. It's Lou."

"That's right, Coffee. You found me."

I turn to see Lou blocking the exit, a tool belt around his waist and a hammer in his hand. "You're Tool."

CHAPTER SEVENTEEN

He grimaces. "See, I never cared for that name. The kids thought they were so clever calling me that. They were all idiots. Every last one of them. Except for Cynthia."

"You're not a private investigator at all. You didn't want to give me the name of your client because you don't have one. You were stalking Cynthia just like you did in high school."

"I didn't think you'd figure that out. And after you found the empty tool belt in Will's shed, I thought for sure you'd stick to the assumption that he was the kid from high school that no one liked. It certainly could have been him. No one he worked with really liked him, not even his students. The only exception was Susan. I'm not sure what she saw in him."

Lou sent Will the tool belt to throw off anyone who might have been on his trail. "I guess you underestimated me."

"What were the odds you'd catch me when I gave you all the information you needed to pin this on Susan and lead you away from me?"

"Well, I guess that's where you went wrong. Never underestimate people with coffee in their veins. The caffeine fuels our brain synapses."

He laughs. "You really are funny. I kind of hate that I'm going to have to kill you."

"Tell me why you were stalking Will." I have to keep him talking so I can figure out a way to get around him and out of this place. He's only armed with a hammer, which means he needs to get close to me to hurt me. But this place is littered with debris, so I can't exactly run anywhere without falling or turning an ankle. If I do either, I'll be as good as dead.

"That wasn't the plan from the start. I came back for Cynthia."

"Did you change your name?"

"Didn't need to. No one remembers me. I was homeschooled until March of my junior year."

"That's why you weren't in the yearbook. You missed class photos."

He nods. "Only one photo of me made it into the yearbook. Not even my name."

"Then your name really is Lou Kershaw."

He laughs. "It is. I only lived in this godawful town for two months. The school didn't think I played well with others. When my parents found all the pictures I had of Cynthia, they pulled me out of school and took me clear across the country. They figured I'd get over my obsession with her."

"But you didn't."

"That's the thing with social media. You don't have to be near someone to watch them. Cynthia posted everything she did."

"Why did you wait so long to come back here?"

"She seemed happy. I never wanted to hurt her in any way. I loved her."

"You didn't actually know her. How can you say you loved her?"

"I knew her better than she knew herself. I knew Will was wrong for her. I saw how unhappy she was even if she didn't realize it. I had to come here. I had to get proof that he was cheating on her, and I did. Except when I tried to tell her…"

"Wait. You actually approached her?" He must have done it Monday morning. "It was you she was looking for when she was in my coffee shop Monday morning. She recognized you from high school."

"I smiled when I saw the recognition in her eyes. She never forgot me."

It's hard to forget the lunatic who stalked you! "She was afraid of you."

"Only because I didn't get the chance to really talk to her. Tell her I was there to help her. Will got out of Susan's car before I could explain."

"You were staying here," I say, looking around. "You went into the car shop after hours and drained the brake fluid." That's why he had the lockpick kit on him. "But why would you tamper with the car if Cynthia was in it? You knew Will and Susan's plan."

"I didn't have a choice." His knuckles turn white, and I know he's tightened his grip on the hammer. Reliving that morning is sending him into a frenzy. "I called her Sunday night and tried to get her to come with me so she wouldn't be anywhere near the car, but she called me crazy and said, 'Leave me alone, Tool.'" His right eye twitches. "I couldn't believe she'd call me that name. Not her. Not after all I'd done for her. And after she ran from me Monday morning when I was willing to give her one more chance..." He raises the hammer and brings it down on top of the pile of broken bricks beside him.

I dart toward the door, but I'm too slow thanks to all the debris on the floor, and he blocks my path.

"Where do you think you're going, Coffee? I'm not finished with you. You're the last step in me getting away with the perfect crime."

"You didn't get away with it. I figured out it was you."

"You can't arrest me, though. And I'm afraid you'll be dead before you get the chance to tell anyone what you know. Without you, the police won't trace anything back to me."

I need to get someone's attention because there is no way to get past Lou on my own. There's only one thing I can think to do. I scream at the top of my lungs.

Lou lounges for me, hammer raised to silence me for good.

I stumble backward, using the counters to keep myself upright. I keep screaming in the hopes that someone will hear, but with the road blocked off, it's probably a futile effort. I grab a broken brick and chuck it at Lou's head, but he dodges it.

"That's how you want to play?" Lou asks. He grabs a brick and throws it at me. I twist my body to avoid being hit, and it makes contact with my left shoulder.

I scream again as I duck around the island, keeping it between us.

He laughs. "Where do you think you're going to go, Coffee?" He reaches across the island, swinging the hammer at me, and I do the stupidest thing. I grab the head of the hammer.

He yanks it forward, pulling me to him so I'm lying across the countertop. I don't let go of the hammer, so he can't hit me with it, but he can still hurt me plenty. He reaches for my neck, but I roll to the side, still gripping the hammer, it comes free from his hand as I go falling off the side of the island. If there wasn't so much debris on the ground, I probably could have stuck the landing. But instead, my foot wedges between bricks, pinning me in place.

"What are you going to do now?" Lou asks.

I swallow hard, knowing I might have to use this hammer on his head to get out of here alive. He advances on me, and I scream again.

"Freeze!"

I don't take my eyes off Lou because I recognize Quentin's voice. "It's over Lou. You're not getting away with killing Will Townsend. And whether or not he planned to kill Cynthia, her death is on your hands, too."

Lou drops to his knees, which has to hurt considering he lands on broken bricks. "No. I loved her."

Quentin makes his way to Lou and cuffs him before asking me, "Are you alright?"

"My foot is stuck and I got hit with a brick, but I'll live." I grab my phone and text Cam to come to his old kitchen.

"Only you would text your boyfriend before freeing yourself," Quentin says.

"Well, I don't see you helping me out of here."

"I do believe I just saved your life. Again."

"Dare I say you treat me better now that we're broken up than you did when we were together. How did you find me?"

"Despite what you think, I do know you. You wanted to solve the case before I did, so I figured you'd return to the scene of the crime to look for clues. I was outside when I heard voices coming from in here." Quentin dips his head at Lou. "I'm guessing you know this guy somehow."

"Yeah, he told me he was a private investigator hired to prove Will was having an affair with Susan."

"He led you to Susan to hopefully keep us from catching him. Did I get that right?" Quentin asks Lou.

"She was supposed to love me," Lou says.

"Yeah, well, he was supposed to love me." I dip my head in Quentin's direction. "Life doesn't always work out the way you plan," I say.

Cam pokes his head into the space. "Jo?"

"Over here." I wave to him. "I could use a little help."

He gets to me as quickly as he can in this mess and helps to dislodge my foot.

"But you see, Lou, sometimes things don't work out for a reason. Like something better is going to come along." I wrap my arm around Cam's shoulder, and he supports me around my waist. "I got a much better guy in the end."

"Let's go," Quentin says, pushing Lou toward the exit.

"What happened to going to Mo's office?" Cam asks me.

"Let's just say I wound up solving the case by accident."

"Only you, Jo. Only you. Let's get you checked out, and you can tell me all about it."

EPILOGUE

8 DAYS LATER

Cam and I are standing outside the newly remodeled Cup of Jo bright and early for the morning rush. The remodel turned out to be better than I could have imagined. We now have ten small tables, several display cases for baked goods, an entire area of just flavored coffees, a huge selection of chocolate, including the ever popular chocolate sticks to put in the drinks, and of course my made-to-order coffee specialty drinks. We put the Cam's Kitchen sign above the window to the kitchen, and I took the most adorable picture of Cam in that window.

"Ready?" he asks me.

"So ready. Let's do this." I turn to address the crowd on the sidewalk. "Everyone, I'd like to officially welcome you to the grand reopening of Cup of Jo, featuring Cam's Kitchen." I open the door to let them inside.

Jamar is inside, wearing a Cup of Jo T-shirt I had

made for him. He greets people before hurrying behind the counter to start taking orders. I still have to hire another employee to help make drinks, but we're off to a good start.

"How many grand openings do you two plan to have?" Mo asks. "Notice Lance only needed the one."

I turn to see her with Wes and Lance. "Hey, guys. Thanks for coming."

"Like we'd miss it," Lance says.

"You, my friend, are welcome to yell and make a scene to get back at me," I tell Lance.

He looks around and scratches his chin. "I think I'll hold on to that card. There's no one here I want to argue with."

"Okay, you save it for another time," I say.

The door behind them opens, and Samantha walks in.

Lance leans toward me. "On second thought, I'm passing my card on to you. You might need it." He gives me a smile before following Mo and Wes to the counter to place their orders.

"Hi," Samantha says. "I won't stay. I just wanted to congratulate you and Cam. I'm really happy for you both."

Cam wraps his arm around my waist. "Thanks, Sam." I'm sure he's answering for us because he thinks I'm not up for talking to her, but I'm surprisingly okay.

"Feel free to order something. Like I said before,

you're welcome here. Everyone is, so relay that to Quentin for me."

"He told me he saved your life."

"He did."

"I guess now that he's saved you twice, you probably don't hate him as much anymore. I just wish there was something I could do to make you not hate me."

"I don't hate you. I don't hate either of you. I just need you to understand that things can't ever be the way they were."

"But you and Quentin were my best friends."

"I know. It's awful to lose a friend. I lost one I really thought had my back."

She sniffles and nods. "I know we aren't friends anymore, but I will have your back if you ever need me to."

I nod.

"Hey, Jo," Mickey says. "I can't tell you how happy I am that you reopened."

"Thanks, Mickey. I'm happy about it, too." I turn my head back to Samantha, but she's already gone.

"I just ordered a chocolate chip scone and a cappuccino. Jamar said you're the cappuccino queen, so he asked me to get you for him."

I laugh. "I've got it."

"I'm going to warm that scone for you," Cam tells Mickey.

"It's like I'm a celebrity or something with this treatment." He follows me to the counter.

"Well, you do have the name of a celebrity," I say, grabbing a mug since I know Mickey will stay to eat his breakfast.

He laughs. "I do! I'm a little bigger than a mouse, though," he adds with a wink.

The place fills up. Most people still take their coffees and pastries to go, but the tables are just about full as well.

"I put another tray of scones in the oven," Cam says. "I can't believe how many we've sold already."

"See, we just needed to partner up," I tell him.

"I always knew that. You were the one who took so long to see it," he says, winking to let me know he's not talking about being business partners.

I smile at Cam and wrap my arms around his neck. "This is definitely the start of something really good." I give him a kiss but pull away when I see Quentin walk in.

He comes over to us. "Congratulations, you two. Almost everyone I passed on the street on the way here had a to-go cup or pastry bag from Cup of Jo."

"That's what we like to hear," I say.

Cam clears his throat. "I never thanked you for saving Jo's life." He extends his hand to Quentin.

Quentin shakes it. "I suppose I owed her since she solved another case for me."

I smirk. "We'll call it even then?"

He nods and goes up to the counter to place his order.

"I think you're right about needing to hire one more person to help out in here," Cam says.

"I know. I'll start taking applications tomorrow. I don't plan to get wound up in any more murder investigations before then," I tease.

"Please don't." Cam wraps his arms around my waist and stares at me.

"What are you thinking?" I ask.

"You are amazing, Joanna Coffee."

Mickey turns to us. "That she is." He raises his cup in the air. "To Jo. She makes the best coffee, and she's the best detective in town!"

"Hear, hear!" rings through the room, but my eyes go to Quentin, who's walking out, his to-go cup slightly raised.

"Did he just agree?" Cam asks me.

"I think he did."

If you enjoyed the book, please consider leaving a review. And look for *Frappes and Fatalities*, coming soon!

You can stay up-to-date on all of Kelly's releases by subscribing to her newsletter: http://bit.ly/2pvYT07

ALSO BY USA TODAY BESTSELLING
AUTHOR KELLY HASHWAY

Cup of Jo Mystery Series

Coffee and Crime

Macchiatos and Murder

Cappuccinos and Corpses

Piper Ashwell Psychic P.I. Series

A Sight For Psychic Eyes

A Vision A Day Keeps the Killer Away

Read Between the Crimes

Drastic Crimes Call for Drastic Insights

You Can't Judge a Crime by its Aura

Fortune Favors the Felon

Murder is a Premonition Best Served Cold

It's Beginning to Look a Lot Like Murder

Good Visions Make Good Cases (Novella collection)

A Jailbird in the Vision Is Worth Two In The Prison

Great Crimes Read Alike

Madison Kramer Mystery Series

Manuscripts and Murder

Sequels and Serial Killers

Fiction and Felonies

WRITING AS USA TODAY
BESTSELLING AUTHOR ASHELYN
DRAKE

The Time for Us
Second Chance Summer
It Was Always You (Love Chronicles #1)
I Belong With You (Love Chronicles #2)
Since I Found You (Love Chronicles #3)
Reignited
After Loving You (New Adult romance)
Campus Crush (New Adult romance)
Falling For You (Free prequel to *Perfect For You*)
Perfect For You (Young Adult contemporary romance)
Our Little Secret (Young Adult contemporary romance)

ACKNOWLEDGMENTS

As always, thank you to my editor, Patricia Bradley. I love how eager you always are to work on the next book, and your feedback is incredible. Thank you to my cover designer, Ali Winters, at Red Umbrella Graphic Designs for creating yet another beautiful cover and for being so easy to work with.

Thank you to my family for not only asking about my books and putting up with my craziness when I'm drafting but for wanting to read the books as well.

Big thanks to my readers, my ARC team, and my VIP reader group, Kelly's Cozy Corner, for reading my books so I can keep writing them.

ABOUT THE AUTHOR

Kelly Hashway fully admits to being one of the most accident-prone people on the planet, but luckily, she gets to write about female sleuths who are much more coordinated than she is. Maybe it was growing up watching *Murder, She Wrote* that instilled a love of mystery, but she spends her days writing cozy mysteries. Kelly's also a sucker for first love, which is why she writes romance under the pen name Ashelyn Drake. When she's not writing, Kelly works as an editor and also as Mom, which she believes is a job title that deserves to be capitalized.

facebook.com/KellyHashwayCozyMysteryAuthor

twitter.com/kellyhashway

instagram.com/khashway

bookbub.com/authors/kelly-hashway

CPSIA information can be obtained
at www.ICGtesting.com
Printed in the USA
LVHW031131190221
679380LV00028B/252/J